KISS OF MIDNIGHT

A WOLFGUARD PROTECTORS NOVEL

KIMBER WHITE

NOKAY PRESS LLC

CHAPTER ONE

MILO

A red file. I hadn't done one of these in over a year. Catch or kill.

I stayed hidden among the trees and underbrush, quick steps. My paws dug into the ground as I neared the clearing.

The scent of a dozen campfires hit my nose all at once. Roasting meat and marshmallows. Hot dogs. Laughter rose. To the east, I scented a family. The dad was telling light-hearted ghost stories to a group of kids. They were easy. Happy. Completely unaware there was a wolf among them.

But I wasn't here for them.

My prey was further west, downhill. She had her own campfire going and as I approached, her scent grew stronger. Dark magic swirled around her. It had a thick, charred aroma mixed with something else, like incense in a church.

I sat back on my haunches as I got her in my sights. She'd just gone back into the green tent she'd set up thirty feet from the fire. She was the only one here without an RV parked beside her lot. I just saw a beat-up red pick-up truck parked at an angle, blocking any other vehicles from getting too close to her set-up.

She was singing. I couldn't make out the tune, but she was good. She hit a trill that sent a shiver down my spine and made my fur stand up.

I waited. Watched. I heard her rustling around in the tent. The embers of her fire sparked and danced, almost in time with the melody she sang. I wondered if that too was part of her magic.

"You need to be careful with this one," my boss Payne had said. The head of Wolfguard Security, he'd trusted me with some of the firm's most dangerous assignments.

I had a knack for bounty hunting. My cousins preferred what they thought were more sophisticated jobs worthy of members of the Kalenkov wolf pack. Well, we were family, not exactly pack. But my father led the largest, most powerful Russian wolf pack and the name carried weight. He hated that I'd chosen my own path at first, but understood it.

I wasn't born to lead the way he was. I was born to hunt. Alone. Rogue if I had to.

Yes. This job was perfect for me and exactly what I needed to get my head back in the game.

I'd been restless of late. Unsettled. Payne and my cousins worried I'd taken too many chances, got myself needlessly close to danger. My sister piled on. I knew what she thought. She wasn't a shifter herself, but she knew me better than anyone. She wouldn't say it out loud but she worried I had some sort of danger junkie death wish.

"I'm always careful," I'd told Payne when he handed me the red file.

Payne pursed his lips. "She's going to be tricky," he said, gesturing toward the file. "Her own coven couldn't bring her back in."

I'd tucked the file under my arm, not bothering to read it. It didn't matter. Payne paid me to bring my quarry in. I'd never once failed him or the firm.

"You ever come up against a wind mage?" he asked.

I shrugged. "A witch is a witch. What's a little hot air?"

Payne steepled his fingers under his chin. "Your family has had a long history with some of the covens in Russia, haven't they?"

"I haven't lived in Russia since I was a kid," I said. "And there's never been a witch dumb enough to go against the Kalenkovs who lived to brag about it."

Payne regarded me with a cool eye. There was more to the story I wasn't telling, but Payne was shrewd enough not to ask. Plus, with his connections, there's no way he hadn't heard the rumors. Decades ago, a rival wolf pack had ousted my father as pack leader. We'd barely escaped with our lives. We'd only survived at all because my father managed to smuggle my sister, me, my uncle, and two of my cousins out of the country and all the way to Chicago. For twenty years we lived in exile and under the constant threat of assassination. Until my father changed all of that and took back his birthright and power.

But we'd paid the price. The rival pack had hired witches to help them get to us. My mother died trying to protect me all those years ago.

"I need you to keep your head clear on this one," Payne had said. He didn't bring up my family tragedy but I knew it was in the back of his mind. He thought I couldn't be objective, that maybe I was too close to this.

"I know the job, Payne," I said. "And I know how to keep my personal biases out of it."

He nodded. "Good. Like I said, this witch might be tricky. Her name is Nadia Bach. She's caused some trouble within her coven. They're based in Michigan City, along the lake."

"I know the area," I said.

"Right. They believe she's turned dark. So she'll be unpredictable. Her coven believes she murdered one of their elders."

"I don't care about their coven politics," I said. "Just point me in the right direction and I'll do what you pay me to."

Payne's eyes narrowed. I felt his wolf brimming just below the surface like mine.

"She's used dark magic to kill another witch from her own coven, Milo," he said. "You don't come back from that, they tell me. It's like a drug. If she's tasted that kind of power, she'll be hungry for more. So she'll be unpredictable. Consider her armed and extremely dangerous.

Don't take unnecessary risks. They want to question her. I guess there's value to them in finding out who hooked her up to the dark Source."

I shook my head. "Yeah, I don't get the distinction. Dark Source. Light Source. It all comes from the same place. And it was so-called light witches who cursed shifters, Payne. I think it's all just made up to keep us from killing them all on sight."

A thousand years ago, witches and shifters engaged in an all-out war. They'd tried to wipe us out by cursing our kind. It didn't work out how they planned. But the curse succeeded in making female shifters of any kind all but extinct. I could count on one hand the ones I knew of, including my own niece. There was a cure now, but I couldn't even openly discuss that with Payne.

"I get it,' I said, opening the file for the first time. Nadia Bach. It was a grainy shot taken from a distance. She was pumping gas into a partially rusted red pick-up truck.

Pretty, I guess. Long black hair, dark eyes. Small. I tilted my head to the side and studied her.

"Evil wears cut-off jeans, cowboy boots, and a Red Wings jersey, apparently."

"Do not underestimate her," Payne said. "Don't get cocky. Who knows what this chick will do if she feels cornered. And Milo, you know what the red file means."

Catch ... or kill. There was no in-between.

That was a week ago. It took longer to catch up with the witch than I expected. But now I had.

I hunkered down, pressing my belly to the ground.

With the sun long since set, I would blend into the shadows. I was invisible.

Still singing, she came out of the tent. For half a second, I thought she was naked.

My blood stirred. Not naked. But she'd slipped out of her jeans and top and wore only a light pink bra and matching panties. She was thin but toned, with ample tits and a nice round ass. She squatted beside the fire and warmed her hands. She reached up and pulled a tie from her hair, letting it spill over her shoulders in a dark curtain.

Then she started to chant. Latin, maybe?

Two seconds earlier, there hadn't been so much as a light breeze. Now though, her hair lifted in a swirling cyclone and the fire rose up in a column. Yet, the air around me remained perfectly still.

Magic.

I bared my fangs, feeling the air thicken. The stench of her magic made it hard to breathe. I nearly bit through my own tongue to hold back the growl.

Saliva dripped from my fangs. I found myself craving the taste of her. A vision flashed before me. This woman. Her hips thrust up as she went down on all fours for me, beckoning me, begging me to take her.

I would devour her. I would snuff out her black magic and bring it into me. The wind around her sounded like a gasp of pleasure as I slipped inside of her.

Shuddering, I side-stepped. The vision cleared and there was only her. She was lying on her side in front of the fire, her eyelids hooded. She was falling asleep. Whatever magic she'd used had faded away. I scented only the woods, the fire, and the normal, almost human, feminine aroma around her.

Her breasts heaved as she let out a sigh. My eyes lingered there for a moment. I drew closer.

She was prettier than I first thought with full, pink lips, the lower more plump than the upper. She had thick, straight brows and a fine dusting of tiny freckles on her chest. She had a birthmark on her shoulder.

So it would be a catch.

I bared my teeth and let out a sigh. She'd fight me, but I was way too strong. Once I tied her hands and blindfolded her, she wouldn't be able to easily cast. And I had a secret weapon.

Tied around my neck, I kept a vial of venom we procured from a cobra shifter. The stuff was potent, but not deadly. One stick of the needle and Nadia Bach would sleep for a day. End of story. Then her coven could deal with her and Wolfguard would get paid.

I stepped out from the shadows, feeling the heat of her fire against my fur.

Nadia's lips parted. Her tongue darted out as she sighed in her sleep.

I took a step toward her and dropped my head to let the rope around my neck fall. The syringe I carried hit the ground and I leaned back, ready to shift. It would only take a second. Nadia would never know what hit her.

I took another step and a tornado rose up from the ground. Dirt and dust choked me and sent me reeling backward. The vial got caught up on the maelstrom and disappeared.

Nadia stood in the center of it, arms raised, eyes flashing then dissolving to purest black. The blast hit me squarely in the chest and knocked me backward.

As I struggled to breathe, Nadia stood over me as the tornado changed course and headed straight for me.

CHAPTER TWO

NADIA

"Crap!"

My booby trap hit the animal squarely in the chest. I'd set up a perimeter around the entire campsite. So far, nothing bigger than a squirrel had tried to get in.

Now, a large gray wolf lay writhing on the ground, his golden eyes fixed in shock.

I scrambled to my feet and lunged toward him, ready to call the wind and take his breath away if I had to. Doing that was risky. Any witch in a hundred-mile radius would sense me. The protection spell was nothing more than a party trick. It would barely register to anyone but me.

And now the wolf.

As I got closer, his back arched and his tongue lolled to the side. He couldn't see me. His central nervous system was rendered momentarily haywire. I had about sixty seconds to figure out what to do.

Ten seconds later, my problem got a hundred times more complicated. He wasn't a regular wolf at all.

As he finally succumbed to the spell and lost consciousness, the wolf's fur bristled then shrank. His claws retracted. Bones and muscles snapped and reformed. The wolf was gone. In its place, I found myself staring down at a well-built, dark-haired, fully naked grown man.

I sank to my knees as my pulse raced. This was bad. A disaster.

"A wolf shifter," I muttered. "Why did you have to be a wolf shifter?"

I reached for him, my fingers trembling; they hovered an inch above his forehead. I had the urge to smooth his dark hair away from his eyes.

He was good-looking. Rugged with a square jaw, full lips, and dark stubble framing his face. He lay on his left side in a fetal position. His calves and quads were massive. I took in every inch, every detail. He had broad hands with rough pads on his fingers. A hard worker. He had ink swirling across his right bicep and more on his chest. A wolf's head with a shield beneath it. The mark was familiar, but I couldn't place it.

"Who the hell are you?" I whispered, then prayed he didn't answer.

I scanned the woods. I wasn't blessed with extra-sensitive hearing like this guy was. I could sense another magic-user well enough, but shifters were something else. And this kind usually traveled in packs.

My pulse skipped. If his buddies were close by, it wouldn't take long for them to figure out something happened to this guy. I knew wolf packs could communicate telepathically. I didn't know if they could sense what happened to him, but if he woke up, he could probably call to them in a second.

"No," I whispered. "No, no, no, no, no."

I ran to the tent and rummaged through my supplies. What I wouldn't give for a little Dragonsteel chain right about now. It was the only surefire way to contain a shifter. Though I'd never had occasion to test it out, I heard it could even keep them from calling to other pack members.

I had nothing that strong here. I'd deemed it far too risky to travel with anything that might draw attention from another witch.

Zip ties. I had plain, plastic zip ties. Without any special ingredient, that wolf could bust through these like paper.

It was better than nothing. I raced back outside. He was still out cold on the ground. I closed my eyes and listened to the wind. Just a little nudge. I couldn't call on too much magic without it acting like a homing beacon to my coven. If I could just use a tiny bit ...

My eyes snapped open. I couldn't be sure, but I didn't hear anything moving in my direction yet.

I grabbed the guy by the heels and started to drag him toward the tent.

"Ooof!" He had to weigh close to two hundred pounds. Dead weight. I was sweating before I moved him even six inches.

With great effort, I got him inside the tent and out of view. I'd picked this particular campsite because it was so far away from all the others. There wasn't much foot traffic out this way and the other renters pretty much left me alone. For the past couple of weeks, I'd just been the crazy hipster lady who hung out at the end of the row.

I zipped the tent flap and started binding the guy's hands and feet. That alone wasn't going to do anything, but I had the germ of an idea.

It wasn't Dragonsteel, but I'd seen the stuff used a couple of times in my life. It gave off a warm glow, a distinct smell, and the weird sensation of having ash in your mouth. I could work with that.

As the shifter started to snore, I set about casting my spell. Luckily, I wouldn't need to connect to The Source for this. I just needed a simple incantation if I remembered the words from the last time I'd read it.

I said them. I think.

The zip ties started to shimmer. For a second, I worried I'd only succeeded in melting the damn things. Then they slowly reformed, thickening. It took about twenty seconds, but at the end of it, they looked just like metal.

I touched one. It was hard and cold beneath my fingertips. The smell was right. I just needed to buy myself a little bit of time.

If I was lucky, I could pack up and disappear before he came to. If I wasn't, maybe I could fool him into thinking his pack was out of reach.

Ten minutes. That's all I needed. I started to stuff my things into my backpack. I'd have to leave the tent behind.

If I were lucky ...

As I turned my back, I felt his eyes staring right through me and knew my luck had just run out.

He was human now, but his growl came through fierce and strong, vibrating through me. I slung my backpack over my shoulder. My jeans and tee-shirt lay in a heap on the floor on the other side of him. I realized how decidedly non-threatening I might look to him sporting nothing but my bra and panties. Plus, there was the fact that he was still completely naked.

"Witch," he hissed. He struggled into a sitting position and his eyes went down to the zip ties.

His lips curled in a snarl as he tilted his head and inspected them.

Please work. Please work. Please work.

It was all an illusion. Barely more than a parlor trick. The bonds would seem strong the first time he tested them. I prayed the look and smell of them would do the rest. If he *believed* they were Dragonsteel, it might be as good as the real thing. At least for now.

"How the hell did you do this?" he asked. His tone was one of curiosity rather than rage. Though that might be the after-effects of the protection spell he'd walked into. It usually rendered animals a little drunk for the first few minutes after they woke up. That said, I'd never hit anyone as big as this guy with it before. I raised a brow. Maybe he was just dumb as a rock.

"You were trespassing," I said. "Serves you right."

"It's a public campground," he said. "In the middle of a state park."

Okay, so maybe not so dumb after all.

I should have turned my back on him and ran for the hills. My thin magic wouldn't work forever. It was a miracle it had gotten me to this point.

"Well," I said. "You're ... a lot."

His face changed. I swear it was almost a smirk. God. He was handsome. Devastatingly so. He had a little cleft in his chin. Maybe I had everything all wrong. Perhaps he was the one using magic, not me. He was a shifter. A dirty, wild, probably murdering shifter. His kind had hunted and killed my kind for centuries.

The moment I thought it, my heart stopped cold. Is that what he was here for? Had the coven resorted to sending a damn wolf shifter after me?

I took a faltering step backward. Run. Hide. Live!

"Relax," he said. "I didn't come here to mess with you. I was just hungry. I smelled your campfire. I smelled ... you. I'd been tracking a deer and ended up in your ... uh ... front yard. There's no reason for any of this."

He lifted his wrists.

"Right," I said. "Except you already think I'm a witch. And I *know* what you are."

He smiled full on at that. "Baby, you're not worth trifling with. I told you. I was just in the wrong place at the right time. But what the hell is someone like you doing with Dragonsteel?"

He kept his wrists out, offering them to me. "It's, uh ... just ... in case ..."

He raised a brow. "In case some rogue shifter just happens to stumble into your camp? Admit it. It's almost like you were expecting me."

I didn't like this. He was too familiar. Too smug. He should be afraid of me. I felt the wind rising. With it, a craving stirred inside of me. It had been so long since I connected to The Source. It beckoned me. It would center me. I could draw strength from it. I missed belonging to something. I missed my brother. Grief hit me like a blow to the chest. I pushed it away.

Since I'd been forced to run for my life, I hadn't dared connect to The Source fully. The coven was expecting that. The moment I did, they'd be able to find me. Then they'd finish what they started. They would turn me to ash but not before trying to get inside my head. My magic was far too valuable to just snuff out with no return on investment.

"A girl can't be too careful," I said. "All kinds of rough types out there. And don't give me your bull about just happening to stumble across my campsite. You knew exactly where you were going. I knew you were out there. Watching me."

He kept that infuriating head tilt. But he didn't deny my observation. The hair raised on the back of my neck. Was he telling the truth? Was he really just some careless lone wolf?

"Listen," he said. "You planning on taking these damn things off me anytime soon?"

"I don't think that's a good idea. I don't trust you."

"Lady," he said. "You dragged me into your tent. If you were that scared you would have taken off in your truck by now. So the way I see it, you either need to unlock this damn Dragonsteel or at least go out there and find my pants!"

I'd done my level best to avoid it all this time. But at the mention of his lack of pants, my eyes flicked straight between his legs.

Mercy. He was huge. Enormous, actually. I'd never really seen a male shifter up close like that. Come to think of it, I'd never been this close to any kind of shifter at all.

I was out of my damn mind. I'd been away from The Source for so long I think it was starting to make me a little crazy. It was the only explanation for everything I'd done in the last half hour. He was right. I should have made myself disappear the second this monster hit the dirt.

It was dangerous to turn my back on him. But I couldn't stand there and stare at his ... member for a second longer. I left the tent and trudged to the tree line. His jeans were easy to find. They hung from a low tree branch just a few yards away from the campsite.

I tore them down and headed back to the tent. My heart jack-hammered inside my chest as I paused at the tent flap. He was still in there. I could feel the heat coming off him from here. It rose my temperature as well.

I went inside and tossed his pants to him. They landed right over his waist, covering the parts that shocked me.

"Great," he said. "Thanks. Think you might unhook the leg bands so I can actually put them on? Or do you have some sort of skirt I could wear?"

His tone was dark, but teasing. I could feel the blush creep into my cheeks.

"I don't trust you," I said. "As far as I'm concerned, you can just hop right on out of here like that. I'm not taking those off. The minute I do you'll have your whole pack down on my head. You know what I am. And I know what your kind does to mine. You trespassed on my space. Not the other way around. As far as I'm concerned, you got what you deserved."

He threw his head back and let out a great sigh. "Baby, you're out of your mind. I'm not waiting to call out to a pack. I'm a nomad. If I were traveling with a pack, they'd have surrounded you about two seconds after you knocked me out cold."

I held my breath for an instant. Was he telling the truth? I wished like hell I knew more about wolf shifters and how their minds worked. I'd just never been anything but repulsed by them before.

"Just … untie me," he said, his voice softer. "I swear I'm not going to do anything. Besides, how do I know you're not about to call a whole coven down on my head? Huh?"

It seemed he knew even less about witches than I did shifters. I was so far outside coven lands it wasn't even funny. The pang of that loss hit me almost as hard as the disconnection from The Source and my ever-present grief for Nicholas.

I don't know if he saw something on my face. But his changed. His eyes narrowed and he moved closer to me.

"You okay?" he asked. "Come to think of it, you don't look well."

He was so close. I imagined I could hear his heart beating right alongside my own. It became overpowering, intoxicating. The heat of him enveloped me and sent a shiver of pleasure straight down to my toes.

It came out of me unbidden. It was as if his nature

called to mine and then, in the same instant, repelled it. He was a shifter. I was a witch, after all. We shouldn't be in the same room together. The little blast of magic shot from my fingertips. Had I done it intentionally, the power of it might have really wounded him. As it was, it caught him off guard and he doubled over and started to cough.

I'd kicked up a blast of dust and he breathed it in. His eyes watered as he worked to clear his lungs. His wolf eyes flashed gold. For a moment, though he'd shift. If he did, he'd know at once the bindings weren't real Dragonsteel at all. Then I was well and truly screwed.

I started to back away. He reached for me, eyes still wild. His hand brushed up against my shoulder, igniting something inside of me.

He caught his breath though his eyes watered. "Nadia," he said. "What the hell did you do to me?"

Nadia.

I scrambled backward, my panic rising. He realized his mistake at last and pulled back.

Nadia. I straightened my back and planted my feet wide, ready to defend myself if it came to it.

"Who are you?" I demanded. "And just how the hell did you know my name?"

CHAPTER THREE

Milo

This woman seemed to be short-circuiting my brain. She stood before me, hands on her hips. I drank in every inch of her. Flat stomach, perfect, full breasts. Her bra and panties fit so well it was like they were painted on. I willed my gaze away from the juncture of her thighs.

"How did you know my name?" she asked again, her eyes sparking with fury.

Well, now I'd done it. Something about her amused me, stirred my wolf. Payne said she was dangerous. Her little booby trap spell definitely got the momentary best of me.

These bindings though. For half a second, I believed they were Dragonsteel. But something wasn't right. They felt odd. When I looked at them, I saw a four-inch band of metal circling my wrists and ankles. But when I pulled against them, they felt thin. Plus, they weren't giving me that dizzy feeling Dragonsteel was supposed to. So it took me about a minute to figure this was nothing more than a trick. A glamor of some sort.

For now, it suited me to play along. Though Nadia seemed more frazzled than evil, I knew better than to underestimate a full-blooded witch.

"I asked," I said, trying to think of a believable lie. "You're right. I didn't randomly stumble on to your campsite. I checked in with the owners before I came out. I wanted to make sure there was no one out here who might cause a problem for a shifter looking to hunt. I asked who was renting the lot closest to the woods. I paid for the information."

She stayed frozen in front of me, hands on hips. I had no earthly clue whether she'd been careless enough to use her real name when she rented the campsite.

"Listen," I said, pressing on. "I know what this looks like. But you've got the advantage. I'm at your mercy."

I lifted my wrists, dangling the fake chains in front of her. How the hell had she done it? It was smart. I had to be smarter. It occurred to me the best way to capture this witch was to let her keep on thinking she was the one who'd captured me. The more I got to know her, the better I'd understand just how dangerous she really was. And I couldn't lie to myself. She was easy on the eyes. It wasn't just my wolf she stirred; it was a healthy dose of lust.

I moved; my jeans slid from my lap. I let out an irritated growl.

"Let me put my damn pants back on," I said.

I expected her to give me a line of bull. But she reacted so quickly, my wolf nearly burst forth. With the flick of her fingertips, the bindings around my ankles separated. They didn't fall off, but I could use my legs. With my wrists still bound, I managed to get my jeans up over my hips.

"Neat trick," I said as I zipped my fly. I had to be careful. Just that little burst of magic and I'd nearly shifted right in front of her. Then she'd know I knew this was no Dragonsteel holding me back.

"Here's what's going to happen," she said. "You're going to walk thirty paces straight out of this tent. If you so much as breathe funny or turn around, the Dragonsteel will be the least of your problems. You're going to count to a hundred, slowly, before you turn around."

She slipped her backpack off her shoulders. Her pile of clothes lay in a heap in the corner of the tent. I couldn't take my eyes off her as she grabbed them and got dressed. "Seems reasonable," I said. "Except for one thing. You leave me out in the woods in these, it might as well be a death sentence. You know what happens to shifters if they're locked in Dragonsteel too long? It'll kill me. Slowly."

"Good," she said, going up on the balls of her feet.

"Lady," I said. "I've never done anything to you except get a little too close to your campfire."

"That's enough," she said. Tiny beads of sweat formed on her upper lip. She was scared. Terrified. I could sense the frantic beating of her pulse. A new sensation poured through me. Never mind self-preservation, I had the overwhelming urge to pop these cheap bindings and wrap my arms around her. I wanted to pull her against me, warm her with my body, and pretty much tear apart anything or anyone who tried to hurt her.

I literally shook my head, trying to clear it. She'd done something to me. It was more than just making zip ties or whatever these were look like shifter-repellant steel. She was practicing some kind of mind control. A filthy spell.

I couldn't keep my wolf completely at bay. I felt my fangs drop. My vision brightened. I knew she could see my wolf eyes glint.

"Watch yourself, wolf," she said. She lifted her hands, aiming her fingertips straight at me.

I snapped my teeth and growled. "Don't."

"Or you'll huff and you'll puff and you'll blow my tent down?" she said.

I squeezed my eyes shut. A vision flashed behind them. I saw myself on top of her. She writhed beneath me, hips thrust upward, back arched.

I was wrong about all of it. Nadia Bach was dangerous indeed. I expected to do battle with fangs, claws, and fists. Instead, this would be a battle over my mind.

"Fine," I said. "If that's what it takes for me to get rid of you."

She came to me, tilting her head; she studied me. I was almost afraid to breathe. I wanted to test the limits of her power. I'd been around witches before. Their magic repulsed me. It reeked with the stench of death and burnt things. I could never understand how humans couldn't smell it.

This witch though. Her scent was heady, almost intoxicating. I expected actual fire and brimstone from her. Not this. Not beauty. Not ... raw sex.

She grabbed my wrists and brought them up. She

turned them, running her fingers over the dark metal. It was the strangest sensation. If I closed my eyes, or looked away, I could just feel that thin plastic. But when I looked in Nadia's eyes, I felt heated metal pressing against my skin.

My wolf snarled. Witch magic. My blood rebelled against it. Oil and water. Fuel and fire.

"Who are you?" she asked.

"Milo," I answered. "My name is Milo. And I told you. I'm a nomad. There's no pack looking for me."

There was, however, something far more dangerous behind me. If I didn't check in with Payne by morning, this witch would have the whole of Wolfguard Security thundering down on her head.

The moment I thought it, a twin urge rose up. The thought of any other wolf getting near her made my blood heat. My fangs were sharp inside my mouth.

"Milo," she repeated. "A wolf named Milo."

She reached up. Her eyes flashed. They were so dark, I could barely make out the contrast between her pupils and irises. I licked my lips past the urge to taste her.

She touched me. Time froze. She trailed her fingertips over the ink on my chest. The Kalenkov wolves, those working for Wolfguard, had all branded ourselves with the firm logo. A wolf's head on a shield. Protectors. Hunters. Guardians.

"I know this," she whispered. "Why do I know this?"

I was a fool to let her get this close to me. Bag and tag. Capture or kill. Payne was clear about my mission here. I had never toyed with a target like this before. I had never even let myself think about it.

I was good at what I did. A machine when I needed to be. Methodical. Stealthy. Deadly. My cousins were good. I was better.

And then a single witch made me careless.

Her eyes flicked upward. I drank in every detail of her. Her lips parted. I felt her soft breath against my chest. My eyes traveled down settling on the swell of her breasts and that dusting of freckles that disappeared beneath the vee of her tee-shirt.

"Milo," she repeated my name. Oh, I wanted to hear her moan when she said it.

My fingers curled, nails turning to claws. It was no good. I was strong. Alpha. The strength of my cold, Siberian bloodline coursed through my veins.

Then, in one instant, this little witch made me lose control.

I growled, letting my fangs drop all the way. The glamor around the zip ties dissolved. Nadia took a step back. Her eyes changed just as mine did, becoming two luminous, black orbs.

"Don't," I warned her, my voice husky with lust and primal rage.

She took a faltering step back and pointed her fingers outward. The wind kicked up, making the walls of the tent vibrate. The flap opened and the cool night air spilled in. The nylon seams gave and the canvas disintegrated around us.

"Nadia," I said, my voice more growl than anything else.

Whatever was happening, it didn't feel like she could

control it. Then a blast of heated air hit me in the chest. The last time, it had been a surprise. This time, I was ready for it.

I dropped low, digging my claws into the ground. Nadia aimed her fingertips at me once more.

I charged her. I just wanted to get my arms around her. I thought if I could block her aim, she wouldn't be able to cast whatever spell she had in mind.

I never even touched her. I got my arms up and tried to grab her. But there was nothing there but cold air.

"Nadia!" I whispered. Though there was a cyclone of activity on Nadia's campsite, the air was deadly still everywhere else. I saw the flickering light of more campfires to the west of me.

Nadia was gone. I saw the contents of the red file in my mind. The source of her power was wind. And now, she'd managed to disappear into thin air.

CHAPTER FOUR

Nadia

Tricks weren't going to work anymore with this wolf. I'd misjudged him. As the swirling chaos of my little spell left him literally in the dust, I left everything behind except my backpack and ran for my truck as fast as I could.

My heart thundered inside my chest. I fumbled with the locks, threw open the driver's-side door, and dove in. From my side mirror, I could see the shifter staggering to his feet. His eyes glowed pure gold as he started to get his bearings.

I dropped my keys as I tried to slide them into the ignition.

Milo stood upright, shoulders back. His muscles rippled as if he were trying to fight off an impending shift.

I found my keys on the floor near my right foot, jammed them into the ignition.

"Come on, come on, come on," I prayed. For once, I

wished I was a fire witch. I would have sparked the engine without the damn keys.

The truck sputtered to life. I smashed it into reverse, tires spinning in the damp, dewy earth. But they found purchase. As Milo started to run toward me, I slammed on the gas and rocketed forward, hitting the dirt road.

I didn't know how fast shifters could run. The odometer edged toward thirty, then forty miles per hour. It was as fast as I could risk going until I hit the main, paved road. As it was, I got some middle fingers and curses thrown at me from other campers as I rounded the camp-site and got the hell out of there.

I didn't see Milo in my rearview mirror. Could I be lucky enough that he'd just given up? He said he just came out here to hunt. He was free now. Maybe I was making way too much out of all of this.

My pulse settled a bit as I made my way out of the campground. There was no going back to it now. I needed a new plan. A new place to hide out.

With each mile I put behind me, my panic eased. Maybe the wolf had been nothing more than a close call. Carelessness on my part. Lord, I'd been on the run for weeks. On my own for months. What the hell had I been thinking dragging that guy back into my tent? I should have just hit the road when he was knocked out cold and been done with it.

I hit the highway. It was early. Dawn would break within the hour. As such, there was barely any other traffic and I'd left the woods well behind me.

I scanned my mirrors and chanced a quick look over my

shoulder. With each passing mile, I felt more confident that I'd overreacted about Milo. He was probably just as happy to be rid of me as I was of him.

Before I knew it, I'd crossed into the next town and the one after that.

The yellow lines of the highway started to blur. My eyelids felt heavy. I hadn't slept since the night before last. I gripped the wheel tighter. I was going to need to find a place to grab a catnap.

As if my truck could read my mind, the low fuel warning light went on. The thing was touchy and mostly inaccurate. The last thing I needed was to run out of gas on the side of the road.

The next road sign indicated I'd find a gas station just two exits ahead. Checking my rearview mirror again, I decided this was probably my best shot.

Feeling halfway normal again, I pulled off. The gas station was well-lit, but mostly empty. There were two semis parked around the back. I might try to tuck my little pick-up in their shadow. First, I lined up to the pump.

Rummaging through my bag, I found my last wad of cash. A quick count made my stomach drop. I was down to five hundred dollars. I could last maybe two weeks on that if I was creative. There would be no more campgrounds or motels though.

As I filled my tank, I pulled out the road map I kept under the passenger seat. I'd left my cell phone behind at my apartment in Michigan City. It would have been too easy for the coven to track me if I held on to it.

I traced the blue veins of the interstate all the way to the tip of the Michigan "mitten."

I had about five hundred miles between Eagle Point and me. It was just a tiny little resort town with a three-digit population. But it was where my brother died.

Acid shot through me. I blinked back tears. In the seven months since I'd gotten word of Nicholas's death I hadn't really let myself openly grieve for him. Once I started, I feared it would drag me down in a black wave of pain. He wouldn't want that. And I couldn't afford it. Not until I could prove once and for all what happened to him. But if they had their way, the coven would never let me get that far.

I folded the map and slid it back under the seat. The gas pump clicked, indicating my tank was full. If I was lucky, I could make it halfway to Eagle Point before I had to fill up again. I wished I could just drive straight through.

Only I knew that's exactly what the coven expected of me.

My stomach growled. I checked my backpack.

"Dammit," I muttered. In my haste to leave the campground, I'd forgotten to throw the last of my food into the bag. It was a costly error I couldn't let myself make again.

I pulled a twenty-dollar bill out of the bag, slid the pack over my shoulder, and headed for the little convenience store attached to the gas station.

I gave the teenage attendant a smile as I made my way to the snack aisle. It would be beef jerky and stale packaged muffins. I grabbed an energy drink and a bottle of water.

The kid at the cash register looked up from his phone to

give me a lopsided smile. The bell rang over the door as two other patrons walked in.

The hairs rose on the back of my neck. I felt something. It was weak, but I had no doubt the new customers were magic users of some kind.

The kid was having some trouble with the cash register. The drawer wouldn't open.

"Hang on," he said. "Sorry about this."

Sweat broke out on my brow. I chanced a look over my shoulder. There were two men. One tall and thin, the other short and stocky. They were talking in murmurs by the beer fridge. I looked up at the round security mirror behind the counter, trying to get a better look.

"Dang it," the kid said, almost shouting it.

"It's fine," I said. "Just keep the change."

"It's more than two dollars," he said.

"It's fine." I grabbed my stuff off the counter and turned. The men by the beer fridge moved. Now I'd have to walk right past them to get out of the store.

My spine tingled. The shorter of the two men was a mage for sure. He was looking at his companion but his posture was anything but relaxed. He stood with his fists clenched, his back rod straight.

I turned to the kid. "Is there a back way out of here?" I whispered.

He gave me a confused look. His gaze traveled to the men by the door and the kid's color drained.

"No," I said. "There's no problem, it's just ..."

"Yeah," he said. "I mean, there's a utility door back by

the restrooms. I mean, you're gonna end up right next to the dumpster but ..."

"Thanks," I said. I stuffed the food I bought into my backpack and walked down the little hallway in the back of the store. I wondered if I should make a stop and wait in the restroom. Would it be more inconspicuous that way?

I heard voices raise behind me. Footsteps on the hard tile floors.

"Hey," the kid said. "Can I help you guys find something?"

They weren't from my coven. If I had to guess, the shorter guy was a fire mage. It would make him volatile, dangerous if cornered. And they might not be here for me at all.

I'd been careful. Other than my little encounter with Milo the wolf shifter, nobody knew where I was. It had been at least two weeks since I'd had any sense of the members of my coven or friends of it. There had only been a close call near Chicago three weeks ago. This had to be a coincidence. It had to be.

Unless ...

The cool air hit my skin as I opened the heavy utility door and walked outside. A black SUV had pulled into the pump station right next to my truck. I couldn't see its driver.

I repositioned my backpack and put my head down as I walked briskly to my truck. I chanced another look over my shoulder. I'd come around the side of the building. The kid was standing near the front entrance. The two men were shouting at him. He flipped the store sign to closed and gestured for them to leave.

I tried to keep my panic at bay. If they followed me, I had to make a plan. What would I need to go up against a fire mage? The other one, the bald guy, was a magic-user too, but I couldn't quite place his source. That probably meant he was an earth mage. They had the most subtle signature of anyone. Earth I could handle. Fire though ...

Bless that kid. He was doing a great job keeping the two suits distracted. But I knew in my gut that fire mage would figure out who I was.

From the corner of my eye, I saw him pull out a piece of paper from his coat pocket. Even from here I knew what it was, and my heart dropped straight down to my boots.

It was a wanted poster the coven had printed on me. They were offering a reward for my capture. A big one.

I heard footsteps behind me. I watched the kid's face go through a series of changes as he read the flyer.

I froze, feeling trapped. I'd slipped between my truck and the gas pump so I knew they couldn't see me. But the dollar signs on that flyer had likely changed the kid's mind about helping me out. I was out of time. All those mages had to do was take a deep breath, and they'd be able to sense my magic like I had theirs. If only I had a way to mask the scent of it, buy myself a few seconds.

"Nadia!"

A deep voice cut through me. The SUV's driver stepped around the back of it.

Milo.

Fully dressed now, he towered over me, his wolf eyes flashing darkly.

The two men started walking toward the gas pumps, scanning the parking lot. They still wouldn't be able to see me from this angle.

If I could mask my scent ...

I rolled the dice.

Instinct fueled me and I grabbed Milo's shirt, pulling him against me. He growled; his muscles went hard as granite. But he didn't pull away.

I felt his heat rising. His wolf eyes flashed. I went up on my tiptoes and pressed my lips to his.

Milo's hands came up. He pulled me against him. His scent swirled around me, heady, intoxicating, totally male, completely feral. Lightning flashed behind my eyes. My pulse quickened and I sensed his beating right alongside it.

An unfamiliar craving rose up inside of me. It was as if my very blood ignited from his touch.

I drew away, gasping. If it weren't for Milo's hands on my arms, I think I would have keeled right over.

A muscle jumped in his jaw. One of the men at the front of the gas station shouted to his companion. They were getting ready to leave.

My gamble worked. Milo's scent was the only thing they could pick out. I might as well have turned invisible. Then I heard the cashier's voice and his words sent a spike of fear through me.

"That's her truck right there."

"Will you help me?" I found myself asking Milo.

His wolf eyes were still glowing gold. I felt his claws lightly scratching my skin.

"Those men," I said. "I think they're here to do me harm. If you drive me to the next town, I'll pay you for it."

Milo let out a low groan and bared his fangs. He looked from the men and back to me. A beat passed between us and my heart nearly pounded right outside of my body.

He reached over and opened the door to the back seat of his SUV.

"Get in," he said, his voice low, menacing. The vibration of it sent a ripple of pleasure through me.

I took a steadying breath, then dove into the back of his vehicle. Out of the frying pan and into the fire.

CHAPTER FIVE

MILO

It wasn't the smartest idea me getting behind the wheel after that. My whole body quaked with the aftershocks of Nadia's skin against mine. I gripped the wheel so hard I'm surprised the thing didn't crumble to dust. I tasted blood in my mouth where my fangs had dropped and I couldn't get it together enough to retract them.

"Who were they?" I asked her. I'd been damn close to ripping the two men at the gas station apart. They wanted her. She'd been right to be scared. I tried not to think too hard about what I would have done if they'd gotten any closer to her.

"I don't know," she said, her voice breathless. From the corner of my eye, I watched her press a thumb against her bottom lip. It was as if she too were still trying to shake off what happened when we got close.

No. This was bad news. She was doing something to me. I expected fire, brimstone, lightning, chaos. Some grand witchy gesture that made her dangerous. I didn't for once think her power over me would be subtle like this. It was like she was in my head.

"Why don't I believe you?" I said. "You knew enough to get the hell out of there and ask for help."

I needed to get in touch with Payne soon. I was starting to suspect Nadia's coven had hedged their bets and hired our competition to bring her in. The second the thought crossed my mind, my wolf raged hot inside of me.

No. No way. I'd rip their damn guts out before I let them get anywhere near this girl. She was mine. My catch.

We were about ten miles outside of Kalamazoo. As soon as I had Nadia Bach secured, I was supposed to take her to a rendezvous point near Jackson. There Payne would arrange for some specialists to help contain her.

Capture or kill. My orders couldn't be more clear. I never bothered to ask what the coven would do to her when they got her back. None of my business. Only now, I found myself caring. Dammit.

"I don't play well with others," she said. "And it's witch business. You wouldn't understand."

"Try me," I said. The second the words were out of my mouth, my head spun. What the hell was I doing asking a target a question like that? It didn't matter. It wasn't my job to sort out guilt or innocence.

"If I asked you about pack business, would you sit here and explain it to me?" she asked. It was a rhetorical question.

"I told you," I said. "I don't have a pack. Not every wolf shifter does. That's a stereotype."

"But you're Alpha," she said. "I don't get it."

"You're not meant to," I said, trying my damndest to go cold. It was her, though. Just being this close to her was doing something to me. More than anything, I just wanted to pull over and wrap my arms around her again.

"Fine," she said. "You're proving my point. You know I'm a witch. I know you're a shifter. I'd say that's all we really need to say about it. The sign back there said we're coming to Kalamazoo in a few minutes. That'll be a perfect place to stop. I can pay you."

"How do you know your friends back there aren't anticipating that move, Nadia?"

She shifted uncomfortably in the seat. "It's not your concern. I know how to take care of myself."

I snorted out a laugh. "Then why are you in my car? You were scared enough you left your truck back there. Not smart. If those two have a brain between them, they'll sit on it, expecting you to come back for it."

She didn't have an answer for me. From where I sat, I could see her eyes start to shine. Damn. The girl was about to cry.

I gripped the wheel even harder. I swear I could feel her heartbeat quickening. But that was impossible. It occurred to me she might be even more dangerous than Payne realized.

We sat in silence for the next few minutes. When the first Kalamazoo exit came up, I blew past it. Nadia didn't notice at first, she was looking behind us.

A few minutes later, she finally realized what I'd done.

"Hey," she said. "You missed the exit." There was an annoyance in her tone, not alarm. Not yet.

"There's nothing in Kalamazoo," I lied. "I've been there. You're better off somewhere bigger, like Jackson. It's only an hour."

"It's out of your way," she said.

"How do you know where I'm going?"

She let out an exasperated sigh. "Fine. Just ... just hurry."

My cell phone vibrated in my pocket. That would be Payne. Sixty miles. If I could keep the girl calm for that long, I'd make it to the next rendezvous point. Payne had already reserved a room under one of my aliases in Jackson. From there, I could call it in. By morning, Nadia Bach would no longer be my problem.

"Relax," I said. "I don't think those assholes are following you anymore. Your little ruse worked. How did you know it would?"

"You stink," she said. "Horribly. Those two were tracking my kind of magic, not yours. I took a gamble that your scent would mask mine. It did."

I laughed. "I don't smell."

"Trust me," she said. "You do. All shifters do."

"Like what?" I asked, my temper rising a bit.

"Woodsy," she said. "Musky. Like ... wet dog times a thousand."

I snorted. "Better than what a witch smells like."

"I beg your pardon?" she said.

"It's thick. Like a hundred bottles of cheap perfume and incense dumped all over you. And there's this burnt smell. Though not on you so much. You're different. Yours is more ... I don't know, airy. That taller guy back at the gas station. He smelled burnt."

"Fire," she said. "His power source is fire. Mine isn't."

I stopped myself from telling her I already knew that. My thin lie about how I knew her name had damn near exposed me. I had to play it far more carefully with this one.

"Anyway," she said. "I don't stink."

She didn't. I was telling the truth about every other witch I'd been near. But not her. Just the opposite. Even now, if I wasn't careful, her scent would overpower me. Sweet, scintillating. It sent a shiver of pleasure through me and settled my wolf. I wanted to wrap myself in it. The truth was, on an elemental level, I craved her.

Oh, she was filled with the most dangerous magic I'd ever encountered. And I was probably the world's biggest fool for not ending this whole thing and calling for reinforcements.

She didn't say much after that. Still, I had the sense that she'd just fed me a line of bull like I fed her. I know what I felt when she flung her arms around me and kissed me. Her skin had warmed to my touch. Her pulse had quickened just like mine did.

We sat in silence for a while. The drive started to calm me. Her too. Part of me wanted to just keep on going. How far could I take her?

"Jackson," she said, snapping me out of the little fantasy I had playing in my head. "Two miles. Don't miss it."

I pressed the accelerator. I was going eighty-five.

"Slow down," Nadia warned. "It won't do either of us any good if you get pulled over."

"So you're on the run from the law now?" I asked. "What the hell did you do, lady?"

"Nothing," she said, her tone sharp, defensive. "I haven't done anything wrong."

I had to remind myself who and what she really was. The red file was tucked under the spare tire in the trunk of my car. I had it memorized anyway. Nadia Bach was a killer. She'd used dark magic to torture and kill a member of her own coven. An elder. I didn't know witch law, but understood it to be the worst sin someone like her could commit.

Would they give her a fair trial? Was that how it worked with witches? Or would I be delivering her death sentence just by turning her back over to them?

"Milo," she said. I damn near missed the exit. I swerved into the right lane, squealing the tires. Nadia gripped the dashboard to keep from toppling over.

"Sorry," I said.

I turned right off the exit. The rendezvous point was just two miles up the road. We weren't staying in Jackson itself but a small suburb. It was a good-sized town but still out of the way. We had a safe house closer to town, but Payne and I thought the motel would suit our needs better. We banked on Nadia's own need for self-preservation kicking in. She'd be less likely to try something big in a heavier populated area. Not that a dark witch would care about collateral damage. It was just more likely to draw attention she wouldn't want.

The Water's Edge Inn had three stories and one main parking lot. That was the other reason we liked it. There was only one way in and out of the place.

I pulled into a space. There'd be a key for me at the front desk. The trick would be getting Nadia into the room without her growing suspicious. I stole a glance at her. She was getting tired. I wondered how long it had been since she'd slept. That could work to my advantage.

"Thank you," she said, reaching behind her to grab her backpack. "This is as good a place as any. I can take care of myself from here."

"You sure about that?" I asked. I realized it was an honest question. Why the hell did I care? The sooner I could touch base with Payne and Wolfguard, the better.

"Yeah," she said. "I'm sure I can find a payphone."

"Nadia," I said. "You don't have a car. Do you even have money?"

"I said I'd pay you for your time," she said. She reached into the outside compartment of her backpack and pulled out a wad of bills. She bit her lip. Her concern was written all over her face. That was probably all the money she had left in the world. I couldn't see it all, but my quick estimation was she held maybe five hundred bucks.

"Here," she said, handing me fifty.

Her fingers grazed mine. How the hell far did she think she'd get on what she had left?

"Look," I said. "I was going to stop for the night

anyway. Why don't you just come with me. I'm not asking you about your business. You just look like you could use a break. Keep your money."

Her eyes flashed. If I had to guess, she was holding back tears. It struck me then she didn't seem like some volatile, deadly, dark witch. She just looked like a scared woman at the end of her rope.

"I can't accept that kind of help from you."

"I don't mind," I said. If I could just get her to the room. I knew we'd reached the moment of truth. If she didn't buy my story, I'd have to take her by force.

She was dangerous. Supposedly evil. She'd killed a defenseless man. I did a mental count of all the charges against her in that red file. I was just doing my job.

"Listen," I said. "If I was planning to hurt you or try anything, I'd have done it by now."

Her lips parted, forming a little 'o.' Damn, all I could think about was how good they tasted. She blinked hard, still fighting tears. Seeing her like that gutted me.

"Why?" she asked.

"Why what?"

"Why are you being so nice to me? I was awful to you."

I shrugged. "Damned if I know." It was the first honest answer I'd given her. I held my breath. Would she go with me easily?

She considered me. My heart thundered. I swore I could feel hers as well. She didn't trust me. But she didn't pull away.

"Thanks," she said.

"Come on," I said. I put a hand on her back. She looked up at me with those luminous dark eyes. Then she let me lead her into the hotel room.

She came easily. But I had a feeling this was about to become the hardest job I'd ever done.

CHAPTER SIX

NADIA

I had a thousand and one reasons not to go with Milo the wolf shifter. He had every reason to have left me to those goons at the gas station. But he didn't. He made me a promise and he kept it. I couldn't remember the last time anyone had ever done that for me. It was that, and the promise of a hot shower and a warm bed that made me cave. If I could just get one good night's sleep, I knew I'd be a different person in the morning.

"You can take whichever bed you want," he said. I walked in behind him. It was a fairly big room for a motel of this kind. Two double beds, a little kitchen area and a massive bathroom with a walk-in shower. It was as close a place like this had to a presidential suite, I figured. And I knew it wouldn't come cheap. I now had only four hundred and fifty dollars to my name.

"Thanks," I said, setting my pack down on the bed nearest to the bathroom.

"I'll go down and order some pizza or something in a minute," he said. "You've got to be starving."

I was but didn't want to admit it. I didn't want to admit I needed anything at all.

I sat down on the edge of the bed and looked up at him. Lord, he was huge. I mean, I knew it before. But somehow, seeing him within the confines of four walls and a ceiling, I could truly appreciate how massive this guy really was. Had I not already known he was a wolf, I might have guessed him for a bear shifter. He had broad, square shoulders that I doubt would even fit through the door if he'd come in straight at it. He had a mass of thick, unruly dark hair that hung just a little too long. I had the impulse to run my fingers through it.

I blinked hard, trying to clear my thoughts of anything like that. It had been that way since the moment he charged into my camp. It was this strange, dual sensation of natural fear for the shifter he was, but also an intense pull to him.

"Nadia," he said, his tone serious, his expression grim. "It might help if you told me who was after you and why."

I rubbed a thumb across the opposite palm. "How would that help?"

He sat down on the other bed. "You're all alone. You're running from something. I'm pretty sure that wad of cash you're carrying is the only thing you have to your name. Did somebody hurt you?"

His nostrils flared.

"Why do you care?" I asked. It came out with a blunter edge than he probably deserved. He really had shown me nothing but kindness.

He put his hands up in surrender. "Listen, I'm not trying to get into your business. I just hate to see a girl like you running scared like this."

"A girl like me." I made a bitter laugh. "Milo, I'm pretty sure you've never, ever met a girl like me."

"Those guys back there," he said. "You say they're not from your coven."

"Nope," I said. "They're the bad guys though. You ever heard of The Ring? I'm pretty sure that's who sent them."

Milo's face went still as stone. I couldn't figure out if it was from recognition. He paused a beat.

"The Ring," he said. "So what do they want with you?"

"So you have heard of them?"

He shrugged. "Maybe. You've been around long enough, you hear lots of things."

"Do yourself a favor and stay far clear of them. They have some funny ideas about our kind."

"Our kind?" he asked.

"Shifters and witches. Other magic users. You may be trying to mind your own business, but they never will. Those men, I sensed magic from them, but I don't know. I think it was borrowed."

"Borrowed? How the hell do you borrow magic?" he asked.

A shudder went through me. I didn't know a good witch who would loan out her power willingly. Men from

The Ring had been known to take it by force. Now that I'd had a chance to think straight, I knew I was right. They weren't natural mages. They were users.

Milo shifted, putting one leg up over the other. "You saying those men want to kill you?"

I stared at the floor. "I think that's the least of what they want from me. They like power, Milo. They want to use it for themselves. I heard about ... some girls once. Got tangled up with men from The Ring and they were never the same again."

"Trafficking?" he asked.

Could he really be that oblivious?

"Something like that," I answered. I'd said too much already.

"So why isn't your coven out here protecting you? I thought that was the main point of being in one."

His words stung. It still hurt to think about what I'd lost going against the coven. I had no choice. I'd been forced into a corner. I'd asked too many questions about what killed my brother. I'd been so stupid not to see the truth right in front of my eyes. Milo was right. The coven should have protected Nicholas. I believed them at first it was a mistake. And then the ground gave way beneath me. Little by little, I started to uncover the lies.

"Turns out I'm not cut out for life inside the coven," I said. "Maybe I'm more like you, Milo. You said not all Alphas have the need to be pack leaders. Well, it's like that with me. What was the word you used? Nomad? That's what I am too."

He furrowed his brow. "Something tells me it's not the same thing at all, Nadia. So, did they kick you out or did you quit?"

"Maybe a little bit of both," I said. It was the truest answer I could give him.

"So," he said. "Where are you going? What's the plan other than crashing here for the night?"

Could I trust him with my truth? Even a day ago, the idea of it would have horrified me.

"My brother died," I found myself saying. "That thing you said, about how the coven is supposed to protect you? Well, you're right. Only they didn't protect him. Now I'd like to know why."

He rubbed his jaw. He had a few days' worth of dark stubble that added to his rugged good looks. I found myself wanting to know what he'd look like with a full beard. Something told me he'd be even sexier.

"Was he murdered?" Milo asked.

"That's what I'm not sure about," I said. "He was living in Eagle Point up near Alpena. Taking a sabbatical from coven life, if you will. After a while, he stopped calling even me. It had been over a month since I'd heard from him. That was unusual for us, to say the least."

"And?"

And what. That was the million-dollar question. Nicholas had just vanished off the face of the earth, as far as I was concerned. Since we were little, we'd been inseparable. Even if we weren't in the same city, I knew I could always reach out to him. As twins, we had a sixth sense about each other. And we were all each other had left in the world. Our parents died when we were teenagers. Nicholas was the only person I trusted and I thought I was that for him.

"He had a heart condition," I said. The words rang hollow to me. It's what the police told me. It's what the doctors said. It was on his death certificate. As his next of kin, they'd given me the autopsy report.

"A heart condition," I repeated. "Aortic dissection is what they said killed him. The kind that even if he'd gone into cardiac arrest on an operating room table, he never would have survived. Congenital. I had to get tested too. We were twins."

My words just tumbled out of me. I hadn't meant to say any of that.

"You're okay?" Milo asked. When I looked up, I saw genuine concern in his eyes.

Absently, I put a hand over my own heart. If I closed my eyes, I could hear it beating. Then, as if beneath it, I heard another. My eyes snapped open. Milo had a look of alarm on his face too.

"Uh ... yeah," I said. "I don't have what Nicholas had."

"Good," Milo said, his shoulders dropping. Then, "But you don't buy it, do you?"

"What?"

"Your brother. You said *they* told you he had a heart condition."

"I don't ... that is ... I still have questions, yes."

"So when did this all happen?"

"Six months ago," I said. "I wanted to go to him. Like I

said, he was living in Eagle Point. He had an apartment there. But the coven took care of it all. They arranged to have his body flown back here for a memorial service. It was ... it was very nice."

Milo grunted. "They're never nice. They're barbaric, if you ask me. It was like that with my mother's too. All the things people say to you. She's in a better place. Maybe God needed another angel. It only ever made me angrier."

I don't know what possessed me to do it, but I reached for him. I took his hand in mine. Milo's skin was so hot to the touch. A shiver of pleasure went through me. I dropped his hand just as quickly and sat back on the opposite bed.

"Well," I said. "I'm sorry that happened to you too. Were you very young when she passed?"

Milo nodded. "I was young, yes. I have a sister too. She's ... not like me."

"Not a shifter," I answered. I knew female shifters were extremely rare. There was something in Milo's eyes. If I had to guess, it was an accusation.

"Right," I said, swallowing. "Not a shifter. And you probably blame me personally for that."

"I don't blame you," he said. "At the same time, I know exactly what it is that witches have done to my kind. I know about the curse. I know your people tried to wipe mine out for centuries."

"And yet here you still are," I said, my tone taking a hard edge. "Are we really going to sit here and list the historical grievances between our people?"

"No," he said, sharply. Then, more softly, "No, It's just,

I was trying to say I'm sorry about your brother. I know that must have been pretty hard to deal with."

"Thank you."

"So now, what, you're on the run from your coven. And from The Ring. Do you think one or the other had something to do with what happened to Nicholas?"

I'd already told him far too much already. "I just don't feel as connected to the coven now that Nicholas is gone. I'd rather be on my own. It suits me."

"And they're not okay with that?"

I wanted to tell him everything. My need to unburden my soul to this near-stranger nearly overwhelmed me. Instead, I folded my hands in my lap and stared at the floor.

"I think I'm just exhausted. It's been a long time since I got to take a real, hot shower. So, if you don't mind, I'm going to do just that."

He smiled. "I don't mind. I'll go ahead and order that pizza. Take all the time you need."

He rose. My gaze traveled upward. I just couldn't figure out why in the hell he was being so nice to me. For some reason, I had the feeling that if I asked him, he'd give me that line from *The Breakfast Club*.

Because you're letting me.

It would have been the truest answer I could give. I *was* letting him be nice to me.

He turned and walked out the door. For the first time in a long time, I was alone with a real roof over my head.

I made good on my promise and headed for the shower. Oh, it was heaven. I let the water run maybe a little too hot. As it sluiced down my naked body, I felt empty inside. I ached. My breath caught as a shudder went through me.

It was Milo.

I wanted him badly.

I wondered what might happen if I just gave into it? It didn't have to mean anything. Just one night. Just to feel a connection to another person for an hour or two. Then, when the sun rose again, I'd be gone.

I already knew how it would feel. Milo would be a generous lover. He'd use those rough hands in the gentlest of ways until he didn't. He had just enough animal inside of him I knew he would bring me to the edge and back again until I was sated and my knees were weak.

A pulse throbbed at the base of my neck. Oh God, how good it would feel. I'd seen him naked. I knew how big and thick he was. My body ached for his touch. Just one kiss had sent me straight to heaven.

I could get it out of my system then. Clear my head. Draw strength and comfort from this man then take it with me as I made my way to Eagle Point. There were answers there for me. I would not let my brother down in death the way I had in life.

Everything had just seemed so neat and clinical in the way they told me he died. I had no concrete proof anything else had gone wrong. But then, the coven sent Michael after me when I started asking questions.

They would try to crucify me for it, but I knew in my heart what Michael aimed to do when I went to see him one last time. And I stopped him. I would stop him again and again in my nightmares.

I stepped out of the shower and found a white plush towel from the rack, wrapping myself in it.

I pushed thoughts of Michael out of my mind and let Milo back in.

It was settled. I would offer myself to Milo and draw from his strength. Then I'd steal away while he slept and seek the truth about Nicholas if it was the last thing I ever did.

CHAPTER SEVEN

MILO

Nadia slept. I couldn't. I paced outside the motel room door waiting for my call to Payne to go through. He was out in the field himself this month on an assignment he wouldn't share details about.

Finally, he came on the line.

"What's the word?" he asked. I looked over my shoulder. Nadia was still dead to the world. God, she was beautiful. Her dark hair spilled over the pillow. She slept on her side, her chest heaving. Her brow furrowed as though she had a bad dream. I had the urge to go to her. I wanted to fight off whatever demons haunted her, even in her imagination.

"Target is in custody," I said. I walked to the end of the sidewalk outside the motel. From there, I had a clear view of the door to our room, but I was far enough away no one would be able to overhear me.

"Good," Payne said. "Where are you?"

"At the rendezvous point," I said. "Just outside of Jackson."

"Okay, I can send a team in or do you have it under control?"

"Under control," I said. "But Payne? There are some things about this girl I think you should know."

"What did you find out?"

"Well, she's running scared. And she's powerful, I can sense that. But I don't think her coven is the only one looking for her."

I gave Payne a brief rundown of what happened at the gas station. He growled on the other end of the phone, not liking what he was hearing.

"You're sure these two were from The Ring?" he asked.

"Pretty sure," I said. "I thought they were mages. Nadia swears they weren't from her coven. She thinks they were just borrowing magic. And she knows about The Ring as well. I played dumb for the most part. So far, she just thinks I'm some well-meaning, a little thick-headed nomad shifter."

Payne chuckled. "She's observant."

"What the hell would The Ring want with her?" I asked. I knew it was nothing good. My cousin and uncle had a few run-ins with their organization.

"I don't like it," Payne said.

"Did you have any idea about their involvement? Do you think her own coven sent them after her? I mean ... like they sent us after her?"

"I'm not sure," Payne said. "Dammit."

"How much do you trust our clients on this one?"

"Less now," Payne said. I was glad to hear it. Something had just not sat right with me about who Nadia was since the second I laid eyes on her.

"Has she tried anything?" Payne asked.

I chewed my bottom lip. I felt a strange loyalty to Nadia. On the other hand, I couldn't forget that I was here to do a job. "She's been cautious," I said. "I get the sense she's purposely not wanting to make any grand magic gestures, you know?"

"That makes sense," Payne said. "I don't claim to be an expert on witches, but I know covens are pretty in tune to who's using what kind of magic within their own kind."

"Right," I said. "She's done little things. She had her campsite booby-trapped. I walked into it. It wasn't that powerful."

"Milo, you need to be careful. She's strong. Our client has said she's one of the strongest witches they've ever produced. You can't trust anything she does. She could be playing you."

His words set my teeth on edge. "Payne," I said. "I can sense her power. But I gotta be honest, more than anything she seems lonely and scared. She's not on some destructive power trip that I can see. And I know where she was headed. At least, I think."

Telling Payne that much oddly felt like a betrayal.

"What do you know?" he asked.

"Her brother," I said. "Sounds like he ran away from the same coven a while ago. He's dead. She thinks it might not have been from natural causes."

Payne was silent for a moment. Then, "Whatever it is, it's coven business. Not ours. This girl has done harm. She used dark magic to kill. If she's done it once, she may do it again. I need to know you're taking every precaution. Where is she now?"

"In the hotel room," I said. "She's asleep."

"Milo, you need to keep one eye open at all times."

"She trusts me," I said. "At least, I think. I mean, enough that she was willing to go to sleep around me."

"Good," he said. "But I need to be honest with you. You sound different. Are you sure you've got a handle on this? Why don't you let me send in an extraction team? They can pick her up and take her off your hands within the hour."

"No!" I said; my voice came out as a growl. "No," I said, calmer. "We do that and someone's liable to get hurt for real. I told you, she seems to trust me at the moment. I'll bring her in. No casualties."

"I trust you, Milo," he said. "You know I wouldn't have sent you out on this job if I didn't."

"Everything has gone off like clockwork so far," I said. "I got her to the motel. She's come willingly. She has no reason to think there's anything wrong. Give me some time. In the meantime, we need more information about who else might be after her. Can you work that from your end?"

"Yeah. I think it's a good idea," he said. "Let me put some feelers out. See if her coven has been double-dealing with The Ring."

"Good."

"All right," he said. "Check back in with me tomorrow night. Keep her there, however you have to."

I gave Payne my word and we hung up. It was nearly dawn. I slipped my cell phone in my back pocket and walked toward the room. I stole a quick glance in the window.

Nadia's bed was empty. My back stiffened. I pulled out the key card and slipped it into the slot. The room was dark and quiet. There was no light on in the bathroom.

"Nadia?" I called out. She had to be here. The door never opened. I'd kept my eyes on it the whole time.

Though I couldn't see her, I sure as hell felt her. The sound of her frantic pulse thundered through me. She was here, she was scared, but the room was empty.

My claws came out and my fangs dropped. I hunched low, ready to shift if I needed to.

There. A shadow moved across the floor. The curtains lifted as if air blasted them from underneath. I blinked. Nadia appeared before me. Her hair blew back, her eyes gleamed.

"What the hell?" I said.

"Who are you?" she asked. "Who are you really?"

"I told you," I said. "My name is Milo."

"Milo," she repeated.

"Nadia," I said. "It's late. You should go back to sleep."

"There's something about you," she said, stepping closer to me. She was different. Her voice had a melodic quality to it as if she weren't fully awake. She brought a hand up. I felt a breeze blow between us.

"Nadia," I said, my voice sharp. Was she sleepwalking?

Her fingers hovered near my face. It was so dark in here still, though I could make out her features clear as day. The high arch to her dark brows, full lips, slightly parted as if she meant me to kiss them. Her nipples peaked beneath the white tank top she wore; I could see the outline of her areolas and every part of me went rigid with desire.

"They sent you to find me," she said. "Didn't they?"

I went still as stone. She still didn't seem all there.

I caught her wrist and her eyes went wide. I felt her blood warm beneath my touch. Her eyes clouded. I grabbed her other wrist. She didn't resist, but her pulse quickened. God. I could hear it beating alongside mine as if it belonged to me. As if *she* belonged to me.

She couldn't. This was a trick. A spell. I knew she was dangerous. But her power didn't seem to manifest in some grand, apocalyptic gesture. No. She was playing with my damn mind. Making me question everything about myself and why I was here.

"They sent you," she said, her voice rising. "Admit it. That phone call you just made."

Had she heard it? How in the hell?

We reached a precipice. Sure, I'd lied to her all along. But she'd lied to me too. Was there another lie I could tell that would reset things back to the way they were even an hour ago?

"Are you one of them?" she asked, her eyes tearing up. I still held her wrists.

"One of who?" I said.

"The Ring. It was too easy. You got away from those two men like it was nothing. They let us get away. That was the plan all along, right? You were supposed to lure me to ... where? Here? Who's coming for me, Milo?"

"Nadia, no one's going to hurt you. I'm not going to hurt you."

She pulled away from me. I let her wrists slip from my fingers.

"But you lied," she said. "You were out for a hunt all right, but you were hunting me!"

I couldn't answer her with words. At that moment, it felt important not to tell her another lie. Silence was the best answer.

A single tear spilled down her cheek. I felt it run across my heart like acid. Oh, she had dark magic, indeed.

A moment passed. Then another.

"I'm not with The Ring," I said. "That, I swear."

"But I'm right," she said. "You were out there looking for me."

I was still shirtless. The first rays of sunshine peeked through the curtains. Nadia tilted her head. She lifted her hand and pressed it flat against my chest, covering my tattoo, the wolf's head over a shield.

"I work for Wolfguard Security," I said.

Blinking hard, she took a step back.

"You're a bounty hunter," she said.

"Yes."

"My coven hired you."

"Yes."

"Did they tell you to kill me?"

I swallowed hard. "If I'd wanted to kill you, you'd already be dead."

She froze. I heard her pulse beating like the second hand on a clock. Tick. Tick.

She faked left then tried to run around me. I moved, blocking her path.

"Nadia," I said.

"Do you know what they'll do to me if I go back there?" she cried.

I hadn't wanted to know. Now, I couldn't stand not knowing.

"They'll kill me," she said. "But not quickly. They'll punish me first. Make an example of me to the others. There's no coming back from what I did. And they won't believe me that I had no choice."

"I'll believe you," I found myself saying. This was insanity. It wasn't my job to weigh the evidence against her. My mission was clear. Capture the target. Bring her back safely. That was it. But this girl upended everything.

"No," she said. "You won't."

She raised her hands. The wind picked up. It was impossible. The door was closed.

Shit.

She was using her magic. Now that she knew I'd been hired by her coven, there was no reason for her not to tap into the source of her power.

I didn't know what she was gearing up to do, I just knew that it would be bad. If I stood still, she would do something she couldn't take back. My wolf would be too strong to contain.

I didn't want to hurt her. But I also didn't want to get flattened by her.

"Stop!" I shouted.

She seemed to be drawing power through her hands. So I took her by the wrists again. I pushed us both backward until we tumbled onto the bed.

I was lying on top of her. Heat rose between us. Her breasts pressed against my chest.

"I don't want to hurt you," I said. "But you're not leaving this room until we sort this out. I'm not your enemy."

I don't know why I said that last part. I only knew I wanted her to believe it.

Her backpack lay on the floor by the bed. I moved off her. Nadia scrambled back up the bed. I found the bundle of zip ties she'd used on me earlier.

"I'm not going to let you go," I said. "But I'm not going to turn you in yet either."

I couldn't believe I was saying it.

She tried to gather her magic again. I felt the air start to leave my lungs. Coughing, I nearly rolled off the bed.

"Stop," I said. "If you try to kill me, you won't have any allies left."

I realized at that moment I truly wanted to be her ally. I wanted to fight off anyone or anything that tried to hurt this woman.

She hit me with something. My eyes watered. The air in my lungs burned. And it was all coming from her hands.

I grabbed her left wrist and snapped the zip tie around it, binding her to the bed frame. I did the same with the other.

Nadia squirmed beneath me but even now, I could feel the growing heat between her legs.

"I'm not going to hurt you!" I yelled. I was still coughing. The burning sensation began to wane though now that Nadia couldn't use her hands to cast whatever spell she'd tried.

"Will you just listen to me?" I said, my voice ragged. "Stand down."

I took a step back. I opened the door and sucked in a great breath of fresh air. It cleared my lungs and my head along with it.

I turned back to Nadia. She looked sexy as hell bound to the bed like that. I shook my head to knock those thoughts loose.

She tested her bindings. They were secure. That sulfur smell dissipated. Whatever magic she tried to use was dormant now. I'd disarmed her. For now.

Only now, I had no earthly idea what I was going to do with her.

CHAPTER EIGHT

Nadia

He'd been lying to me since minute one and I fell for it all. With my hands bound to the bed frame, I couldn't easily throw some wind at him. That didn't mean I was defenseless.

Milo's eyes glinted in the dim light of the hotel room. He was sweating, pacing at the end of the bed, and I could feel the turmoil inside of him. As much as I wanted to let my darker magic out, he wanted to let his wolf out. And oh, I wanted him to.

Even as my anger rose, so did my desire for him. Part of it was the naked lust in his own eyes. I knew what he was. He knew what I was. That alone should have been a reason for us to fight. To recoil from each other. Instead, more than anything else, I wanted to feel his skin on mine again.

Except he'd been sent here to do me harm.

"Will you just listen to me?" he said, snarling.

"You're with them," I said. "Those men at the gas station. We threw them off too easily. They knew who you were. Is that it?"

"No!" he snapped.

He thumped his chest, laying his palm flat over the wolf and shield tattoo on his pectoral muscle.

"I work for Wolfguard Security," he said. "And we've been hired to bring you back."

Rage pooled in my gut along with that inexplicable desire.

"Hired by whom?" I asked, though I was afraid of the answer.

Milo sighed. He tore a hand through his hair as he started pacing again.

"The Ring?" I asked. "My God. That's it, isn't it? Milo, do you know what they are? What they're capable of? You, of all people. The Ring is a bigger threat to shifters than they ever could be to witches."

"Why?" he asked. "What's their agenda?"

I shook my head. "Nothing good. They've been behind some of the worst crimes against shifters. I've heard they backed a powerful *Tyrannous Alpha* in Kentucky."

Milo's face changed. He knew who I meant. For at least twenty years, Kentucky shifters had been controlled by a totalitarian regime. The overthrow of their dictator had only happened recently.

"I know about Kentucky," he said. "My boss was part of the rebellion that took that monster down."

"Then what the hell are you doing working for the people who helped bring him to power?"

Milo shook his head. "We weren't hired by The Ring. I told you. We were hired by your coven."

His words struck me like a physical blow to the chest. My coven. I hadn't wanted to believe it when he said it the first time. They'd allied themselves with shifters against me?

"You've been lied to," I spat. "What did they tell you? That I'm some evil, dark witch who can't be controlled?"

He didn't have to answer. I could see the truth in his eyes. Yes. That's exactly what he'd been told.

"What's the plan?" I asked. "You keep me here and then they come to pick me up?"

He still didn't answer. Only the slightest flicker in his eyes betrayed his emotions.

"They want me dead," I said. "But they're not just going to kill me outright. They'll try to strip me of my power first. I'll die slowly and in agony. If I'm lucky, that is."

He came to me. I wanted to think it was real pain I saw on his face.

God, I'd been such an idiot to trust him this far. He was no witch, but this man had used some kind of magic over me to make me ignore my own instincts.

"I don't want that to happen to you," he said. "You need to believe me that I don't want to hurt you."

I shouldn't. Every single event that had happened had led me to this place. I was right where Milo and my coven wanted me. And yet, here I was searching for ... something ... from this shifter I just met.

"How much did they pay you?" I asked, my tone acidic.

"Nadia ..."

"No, I want to know. How much am I worth to them?"

His shoulders dropped. "I have no idea. I'm sent to do a job and I do it. The details aren't up to me."

I struggled against the bindings. Milo's face lost all color.

"I'm sorry," he said. "I don't want to hurt you."

"You're signing my death warrant," I said.

He reared back as if I'd slapped him.

"Do you have any idea how many rules I've broken? Lines I've crossed?"

"So just get it over with then," I said. "Kill me if you have to. A quick death right here, right now, would be mercy."

He touched my leg. It was as if an electric current shot from him to me. My pulse quickened.

"You are powerful," he said. "I can feel it. Why the hell can I feel it?"

I looked away from him, toward the window. I squeezed my eyes shut. I didn't want to know these things. I didn't want to trust my own heart.

"I've done nothing to you," I finally said, turning to him. "Except trust you."

"They say you killed an elder from your own coven," he said. "They say you eviscerated him."

How could I begin to explain in a way he'd understand? I took a breath.

"It was in self-defense," I said. "I asked too many questions about what happened to my brother."

Milo tilted his head. "You think your coven had something to do with it?"

Should I trust him with the whole story? Did I have any other choice?

"Nicholas was worried about something," I said. "In the last few months before he ran off, he'd grown disillusioned about leadership within the coven. He would never tell me anything in great detail. He was vague. Told me to be careful who I confided in. After a while he stopped making sense at all. He was depressed. Then manic. I wanted to get him some professional help but when I broached the topic, he shut down on me."

Milo listened. His brow furrowed; he kept his eyes locked with mine.

"The day before he took off, he left me a note. He said if anything happened to him, I shouldn't try to find him."

"What about the man you killed?" Milo asked.

"I did everything Nicholas warned me not to," I said. "I was too trusting. It appears to be my main downfall."

Milo winced.

"My parents are dead," I said. "I told you that. I only have an uncle, but he's been exiled from the coven for years. They accused him of trying to use dark magic on a woman he was having an affair with. I never knew the whole story about Uncle Cyrus. He and my father weren't on speaking terms before my dad died. Anyway, our family has been on a watch list ever since. If there's a dark witch in the bloodline, then they think any of us might turn."

"What happened with the man you killed?" he insisted.

"His name was Tolliver," I said. "Michael Tolliver. And he's only dead because he tried to kill me first."

"How?"

I didn't want to relive that night. The fear. The chaos.

"Tolliver told me there was going to be a full meeting with the council. I'd confided my fears about Nicholas to him. Tolliver had at one time been close with my parents. He was kind of like a godfather to us."

"Anyway, Tolliver was the only person I trusted within the coven. But he got sick. With everything that happened with my brother, I started to get suspicious. I thought maybe they were doing something to him because the elders knew he was still close to me. I knew time was running out. I knew it was only a matter of time before they made a decision about what to do with me. I was pretty sure they were getting ready to banish me, or worse."

"Just for asking questions about your brother?" Milo asked.

"Yes. But more than that. I think they were afraid I'd turn dark. Nobody questions the elders like I had. Anyway, Tolliver sent word to me. He wanted me to meet him. He was very sick and I think he knew his days were numbered. So I went. But he was armed."

"What do you mean armed?" Milo asked. His fists clenched.

"He tried to knock me out with a spell," I said. The memory of that night was still seared into my brain. Michael Tolliver tried to cast a spell that would have rendered me completely immobile. Just the very beginnings of it turned my insides to ice.

"He wasn't there to bring me to the council," I said; my voice sounded flat, emotionless.

"He tried to strip me of my power," I said. "I saw his heart that night. He was going to kill me."

"What did you do?" he asked.

"The only thing I could," I answered. "I defended myself. I fought back. I called on the wind and took Tolliver's breath away. I didn't mean to kill him. I only meant to stop him. But ... something went wrong. It got bigger than me. When it was all over, I had no other choice but to run. If Tolliver had been sent by the council, it meant I had no more allies within the coven. And it meant they don't want me to find out what really happened to Nicholas. I can't live with that."

Milo put a hand on my leg. His touch was tender and kind. It could all be another trick.

"I'm sorry that happened to you."

"And you," I said, leveling a hard stare at him. "What did they tell you about me?"

His face turned to stone for a moment. Then he took a breath. "That you're dangerous. That if I couldn't capture you safely, I have orders to kill you."

It went deathly quiet between us. I stopped struggling against the bindings.

"Is that it then?" I said. "You'll kill me?"

His jaw twitched. He spoke a single word and it thundered through me.

"No."

"Then help me," I said. I couldn't believe I was asking. But there was something in Milo's eyes. I was probably a fool for thinking it. He'd lied to me this long. Why should I believe he wasn't now?

"I won't fight you," I said. "You have my word on that. If you let me go to my brother's apartment. I have to know what really happened to him."

"How is going to his apartment going to give you those answers?" he asked.

I took a breath. "Because I know he died there. If I can stand in the place where he drew his last breath, I have the means to see what happened to him."

Milo rose slowly off the bed. "That can't be white magic."

"It's not," I said. "It's about as dark as you can get. But it's the only way."

"And then what?"

I didn't answer.

"Milo," I said. "It's like you said. If you wanted to kill me, you would have done it by now. You've had about a dozen chances. And if I wanted to hurt you ... really hurt you ... I could have. And yet, here we are."

"Here we are," he repeated.

"So help me," I said. "I have nobody else left."

Even as I said it, I felt the faintest echo inside my heart. I wasn't alone anymore. But no, I couldn't give into that kind of insanity. It was desperation. Fight or flight. Milo was a wolf shifter. And I was ... me.

"Do you think I'm bad?" I asked. "You've been with me non-stop for two days. If I was as dark as you've been told, don't you think I would have tried something by now?"

He reared back, launching himself off the bed.

"I think you have." His voice was cold.

He got close to me. His face was no more than an inch from mine. I felt his heat. I felt his heart.

He pressed his hand over my heart, snapped one of the zip ties, and grabbed my hand, placing it over his heart. He closed his eyes. It was almost involuntary, but I did the same.

Our pulses beat in perfect synchrony. If mine quickened, so did his. When calm settled through him, I felt it inside me too. We were connected somehow, though it couldn't be possible.

My eyes snapped open. "You think that's me?" I drew my hand away. "You think I'm making you feel that?"

"Aren't you?"

I dropped my chin meeting his eyes. "No," I said. "I swear. Whatever that is, I'm not doing it."

He snarled. Once again, his wolf played just below the surface. Golden eyes. Claws out.

I didn't know what any of this meant.

"It's not me," I said. "The only spell I've thrown at you was that booby trap back at the camp."

"And now," he said. "Before I bound you. You were trying to hurt me."

I couldn't deny it. "So you wouldn't hurt me first."

His answer tore out of him, almost as if it were involuntary. "I will *never* hurt you!"

Once he'd uttered those words, he staggered backward. He seemed just as surprised by them as I was.

"Milo?" I asked.

He shook his head as if to clear it. "Magic," he whispered. "A damn spell."

"No," I said. "I've cast no spell on you. I swear on my brother's grave. My parents. Everything I've told you in this room is the truth."

He started pacing again.

"Milo," I said. "I give you my word. Take me up to Eagle Point. Let me find out what really happened to my brother. After that, I'll go with you willingly wherever you say. I won't try to fight you. Please. You have all the advantages here. No matter what you think, you're stronger than I am."

He finally stopped pacing and squared his shoulders. I could see the war going on inside him behind those glinting wolf eyes.

"Eagle Point."

"Yes," I said. "It's about two hundred and fifty miles. I have no one else to turn to."

"Dammit," he muttered. "I think I'm losing my damn mind."

But I'd won. I could sense it in him. My heart lifted.

He came back to the bed. His index finger was a claw. He used it to slice through the second zip tie, freeing me. I rubbed my wrist.

"Come on," he said. "If we're going to make Eagle Point by the end of the day, we'd better get a move on."

I scrambled off the bed after him and grabbed my backpack on the way out the door.

CHAPTER NINE

MILO

"You're going to what?"

Nadia sat in the passenger seat of the SUV. She stared straight ahead, her skin pale. I did my level best to explain to Payne what I'd decided.

"I need you to call off the extraction team," I said. "I'm going to deal with this myself. I think we've been lied to."

"Milo," he said. "What makes you think this whole thing isn't a setup? We have no idea what kind of power that witch can wield. I told you I'm trying to get more information and I am. You need to stick to the plan and bring her in. Let her coven decide what to do with her."

"Payne," I said. "I know what you're thinking. Three days ago, I'd have thought it too. But some of what she says makes sense. Can you do something for me? Find out more about this elder witch she supposedly killed. Nadia swears it was in self-defense. She thinks her brother, Nicholas, was close to finding out some secret about their coven they didn't want to be revealed. She thinks they killed him for it and sent this Tolliver to make sure she stayed quiet too."

Payne let out an audible sigh.

"I don't like it," he said.

"I know. And I also know what this probably sounds like. But ... I've spent some time with this woman. I sense that she's desperate. She's in deep grief. But she's not evil, Payne."

"I don't want you walking into this thing by yourself," he said. "At least let me send some men to meet you."

I bristled. The thought of any other shifters being around Nadia made every protective instinct I had flare. But there was no arguing Payne's logic.

"Fine," I said. "But let it be Kalenkov men. Pull Edward and Erik off whatever they're on and have them meet me. I'll text them where."

Erik and Edward were my cousins. Along with my Uncle Val and cousin, Leo, they were the men I could trust with my life.

"All right," Payne said. My heart settled. I figured he'd put up more of a fight on this one.

"What is her plan, Milo?" Payne asked.

"She thinks she'll be able to see what happened during her brother's last moments. It's ... hard to explain. Witch shit. That's all I can tell you."

Payne made a noise. I could almost see him rubbing a hand down his face on the other end of the phone.

"You have to trust me that I've got this one under control."

"Do you?" Payne yelled. "Because you haven't been acting like yourself since the second you made contact with this witch. How do you know she isn't using magic on you right now?"

I stopped cold. I couldn't say it. Couldn't admit it to myself, much less Payne. But with each second that passed, I knew there *was* magic at play between Nadia and me. Only it wasn't a spell.

There was only one thing that could make me sense her fear like that. Feel her pulse beating in time with mine. And the attraction I felt for her nearly drove all reason from my head. I wanted her. I craved her. And she was a damned witch!

"Two days," Payne said. "You can have forty-eight hours to see if this little story of this Bach woman pans out."

"What about those men I told you about?" I asked. "The ones Nadia thinks are working for The Ring?"

"I've given their descriptions to another operative of mine. They haven't been seen since. We talked to the owner of the gas station and had him pull the security footage. They aren't from Nadia's coven. That's the only thing I know for sure."

"Payne," I said. "We know what these men from The Ring are capable of. They've been actively procuring women and trafficking them to powerful men."

Wolfguard's first run-in with The Ring happened when my Uncle Val was sent to guard a woman engaged to one such powerful man. He ended up saving her from an awful fate and now Val and Willow were married.

Fated mates.

I hadn't really allowed myself to think that far ahead. But everything I'd felt since I met Nadia could mean just that.

"Just see what you can find out about this Nicholas Bach," Payne said. "I'll keep working it from this end too."

"Payne," I said. "We have to prepare for the possibility that Nadia's coven is working with The Ring. I can feel it in my gut. I think that's who sent those two men to try and nab her at the gas station. If I'm right, the fewer people who know she's still with me, the better."

"Milo," he said. "Just watch your back. You get so much as a sense that raises a hair on the back of your neck ... don't wait. You send for backup. If it means leaving Nadia behind ..."

I swallowed hard. I didn't have the heart to tell him that was never going to happen. I was in this far too deeply with her now to back out.

"Got it," I said, lying and hating myself for it. But I knew I'd gotten as much from Payne as I was going to. And it was a lot. It would be good to have my cousins working this case with me. I only hoped it wouldn't spook Nadia into doing something crazy.

We hung up and I headed back to the SUV. Nadia gave me a wary smile as I slipped behind the wheel.

"Well?" she asked.

"We're a go," I answered. "I'll go with you to Eagle Point. I'll make sure nothing happens to you while you do ... whatever it is you're planning to do. But if there's even an inkling of trouble ..."

She put a hand up. "I know. And there won't be. Not

from me. I swear it. Thank you, Milo. You have every reason not to trust me on this."

"The sooner we get this little side trip over, the better," I said, putting the car in gear.

Nadia clicked her seatbelt in place as I pulled out of the hotel parking lot and headed northeast to Eagle Point. If traffic stayed clear, we'd be there in four hours or less if I drove straight through. But that wasn't the plan.

We sat in companionable silence for a while. Finally, I turned to her.

"Nadia," I said. "How do you know your coven isn't expecting you to go straight back to your brother's apartment?"

She picked at a cuticle. "I don't," she said. "I only know that I'll be able to sense them if they get close. Er ... probably."

"Probably?" I said, nearly losing control of the wheel. We swerved a bit to the right before I recovered.

"Yes," she said, defiant. "Probably. I'm just as eager to get this over with as you are. The last six months have been sheer hell for me. And you're oddly the first person I've told any of this to. I've been on my own. Alone. And I know the risk this puts you in. I've been living with that risk the whole time. Look what it's gotten me."

I gripped the wheel and stared straight ahead.

"It's gotten me you," she said. "Have you ever stopped to think how desperate my coven is that they resorted to hiring a group of shifters to find me?"

I didn't answer. I couldn't. It was a question I'd been asking myself over and over. God, my life was so much easier when I just thought of her as quarry I'd been hired to bring in.

"What was he like?" I asked. "Your brother."

Nadia sat straighter in her seat. "Brilliant," she answered. "He could have been anything he wanted. A rocket scientist. An astronaut. A neurosurgeon. He was gifted and kind. And he was so much better than I am."

"Why do you think that?" I asked.

"I didn't want this," she said, lifting her hands. "All this power. My whole life I've had to hear about my family's legacy. Bachs are descended from the original wind mages. There's been a Bach seated among the council for as far back as anyone can remember. Then my father died. Then my uncle turned his back on the coven. Or they turned their backs on him. Depends on who you ask. Then Nicholas did the same. So it was all supposed to be on me. To carry on the family name and all that. Except I was never good at it."

"Nadia," I said. "You're good at it. Believe me."

She turned to me. "What are you talking about?"

I hesitated. How could I tell her that the weapons she tried to use against me—power that only seemed to come from her hands or her sheer force of will—had nearly knocked me flat? Me. An Alpha. A Kalenkov.

"I just wanted to be normal," she said. "With the council, all I've ever seen is backbiting and politics; who needs it? It's not for me. Only I'm stuck with it. And there's something wrong with it all anyway. It's why Nicholas left."

Her hair started to lift from her shoulders. She was giving off power right now and she didn't seem fully aware of it. I was having a hard time keeping the car from veering off the road. The winds around us were so strong, my tires locked.

"Nadia!" I shouted. Instinctively, I reached for her. I took her hand in mine and she calmed. Her hair fell back into place. The trees bordering the road stopped bending.

She buried her face in her hands. "You see? That's what always happens. That's how it's so easy for them to figure out where I am."

"But you stopped it," I said. "And it's part of who you are. Just like the wolf is part of me. It's our nature. And it belongs."

She was staring straight at me, tears threatening to fall from her eyes.

"I've never belonged anywhere, Milo. Not once."

I felt her loneliness in my own heart. It was hollow and cold, but at the center of it, I felt a growing heat. She was so familiar. As if I'd known her in a dream or met her once, long ago. Nadia felt like ... home.

"How much farther?" she asked.

"A couple of hours," I said. "I'm going to stay off the main highways between here and Eagle Point. I like keeping the woods close enough that I can smell it."

She nodded and yawned. My stomach growled. It was nearly dinner time and we hadn't bothered to stop for food.

I came to an exit showing signs to a truck stop. It was as good a place as any to grab a quick bite before we continued on.

Nadia caught my thinking and slid the straps of her backpack over her shoulders. I realized it was all she had left to her name. She'd left everything behind. Finding the truth about her brother had been worth it to her to give up her entire life.

The diner was just a greasy spoon but the scents coming from the kitchen were heavenly. We each ordered the cheeseburger platter and devoured it as soon as the waitress set it in front of us.

I enjoyed watching Nadia eat. Hell, I enjoyed watching everything about her. I still couldn't bring myself to broach the subject of what that all meant.

Did she understand about fated mates? I knew she felt something too. But her coven had been so prejudiced against shifters, it was hard telling what she might think of it all. I still wasn't sure what I thought of it all. It could still be a trick. Some protection spell she cast to get me to forget who I was around her. Only it felt so good, I wasn't sure I minded.

I dipped the last of my fries in ketchup and polished them off.

"Tell me about Wolfguard," she asked. "Is bounty hunting what you do for them all the time?"

I cleared my throat. Most of the answer to that was public knowledge if someone cared to look.

"Mostly," I answered.

"And you're good at it," she said. "I'm guessing very good."

I leveled a stare at her. "I'm the best there is."

She shrugged. "Well, you found me easily enough. Why do you suppose that is?"

I folded my napkin on my plate and draped an arm over

the back of the booth. "It's just something I was born to. It suits me more than leading a pack. I suppose that's something we have in common then. I never had any inclination to be pack leader like my father is."

"Is he your pack leader?" she asked.

I shook my head. "No. The Kalenkov pack is in Russia. I go back there from time to time, but I don't belong to it."

"What happens after your dad ... I mean ... when he isn't able to run it anymore?"

I looked out the window. The sun had already set. I decided we'd be better off tackling whatever Nadia needed to do by the light of the day. So we'd need a place to hole up for the night.

I'd spotted a sign for lodgings just a mile down the road. Though it was tempting to head straight to Nicholas Bach's apartment, I wanted a fresh head when we did it. And I'd promised Payne I'd wait for my cousins to arrive. I wondered how Nadia would take to their presence. I hadn't brought myself to tell her yet.

"He'll choose another wolf native to Russia, probably," I answered. "I was born there but haven't lived in the mother country since I was a boy. America is my home now. I belong here."

"And how does your dad feel about that?" Nadia sipped through her straw.

"He understands. He believes we all need to follow our true fates, wherever that takes us."

Nadia's eyes flickered. My true fate. I knew in my heart I might be staring right into it. Impossible as that may seem.

"Well, he sounds like quite a guy then, your father.

Mine put more stock in duty than fate. But look where that got him."

"I'm sorry for your loss, Nadia. I lost my mother too."

I hadn't meant for my words to take a hard edge, but they did, and Nadia picked up on it.

"Witches," she whispered as if she could read my mind. "They took her from you."

"They helped," I said.

"I'm sorry for that," she said. "The thing is, you'll know a truly dark witch when you see one."

There was a challenge to her words. She kept her eyes locked with mine. Was I seeing one now?

She was powerful. Deadly, even. And she'd used those powers to kill at least once by her own admission. But was she truly dark?

I accepted her challenge. Reaching across the table, I took her hand in mine. Her skin was warm to the touch. Her pupils dilated as she stared at me. She felt so good. That little jolt of electricity between us warmed my heart.

I sensed power, rage, desperation, loneliness. But also fierce strength and the edges of her grief. Nadia Bach was a lot of things, but I was willing to bet my life she wasn't as dark as they said she was.

Her breath caught. For a second, a breeze lifted her hair. Then she blew it out; settling back against her booth she slid her hand from mine.

"What was that?" she asked.

How could she not know? What had her coven told her? And why couldn't I bring myself to say the words out loud even now?

Fate. Destiny. My wolf answered for me.

Mine. She belongs to me!

I opened my wallet and put two twenties on the table.

"Come on," I said, letting the moment pass. "We'll crash for the night and head to your brother's first thing in the morning. I just hope you can handle whatever answers you find there."

She took one last sip of her drink and followed me out. Her breath blew hot beside me.

Fate. Destiny. In my heart I knew the darkest of her magic was yet to come.

CHAPTER TEN

Nadia

Nicholas had rented a small house just outside of Eagle Point near Alpena. It was in the northeast edge of Michigan on Lake Huron. Beautiful country within the Atlanta State Forest area. I'd never been there before but would have been able to find it better than any GPS. It was as if he was guiding me to it and I wondered if Nicholas had cast some sort of location spell before he died.

I sat in the passenger seat of Milo's SUV. He was stoic, scanning the street. We'd parked down from the house at an abandoned gas station.

Wolfguard Security. I'd been foolish to trust him. And yet, part of me still did. He'd brought me this far. If Milo intended to turn me over to the coven outright, he could have done it days ago.

But he hadn't. He'd driven me on my harebrained

scheme to see if I could find any answers about what happened to Nicholas.

Now he wouldn't let me leave the car.

"Milo," I said, trying to keep the desperation out of my voice. "The longer we wait here, the more likely somebody's going to figure out I've come."

He clenched his jaw and tapped his fingers on the steering wheel. "I don't like it. We should leave."

"Do you sense something? More shifters?"

"No," he said. "It's just ... I don't know."

I reached for the latch on my seatbelt and unhooked it. If I tried to get out of the car now, would he stop me?

"We should do this now," I said. "I need ten minutes. That's all. If Nicholas left anything behind, it shouldn't take me more than that to find it. You can tie my hands up again if you want to."

His eyes flashed. I couldn't read him. Was that guilt or desire?

He pulled out his phone and made a call. He spoke in short, clipped sentences.

"How long?" he asked. I could tell from the line in his brow he didn't like the answer. He clicked off the call and turned to me.

"Okay," he said. "Here's how this is going to work. I'm going in there with you. I catch so much as a whiff of anything wrong, we're out. I don't care if you haven't found what you're looking for. I'm out of my damn mind taking you even this far."

So why are you? I wanted to ask. But I wasn't sure I was ready for his answer.

"Deal," I said. I opened the passenger door, not wanting to give him a chance to change his mind.

Milo moved quickly. He had a hand on my lower back. His eyes darted back and forth. They glinted as he let just enough of his wolf out, ready to shift in an instant if trouble came.

I listened for it too, stretching out my own sixth sense. But everything on the street seemed calm and normal.

We got to the front door of Nicholas's apartment. There was a For Rent sign in front. It was a two-story brick house and Nicholas had lived on the first floor. I'd only been here one other time, right after he moved in.

I reached into the side zippered compartment of my backpack and pulled out the single key he'd given me, hoping he hadn't changed the locks.

"It's been six months," Milo said. "What makes you think any of your brother's stuff is even still here?"

"Because he paid the rent in advance for the whole year," I said. "The coven arranged for his things to be sent back home, but no one's supposed to be living here until the first of the year. Not on the first floor anyway. That sign is probably for the upper unit."

I said a silent prayer as I tried the key in the lock. It fit. The latch opened. I shot Milo a look that said, "I told you so." Then I stepped inside.

It was a huge, open space. A large living area with a kitchen off to one side. Hardwood floors throughout leading to a single hallway to Nicholas's bedroom and adjoining bath.

Our footsteps echoed off the walls with no carpet or

furniture to absorb the sound. It felt cold, drafty, and lonely, But beneath all of that, I still sensed something of Nicholas. It brought stinging tears to my eyes.

"Do you know where it happened?" Milo asked, whispering as if we were walking through a graveyard. In a sense, we were.

I closed my eyes. *Where are you?*

"Do you sense anything?" Milo asked.

"Do you?" I asked him.

I opened my eyes just as Milo closed his. His nostrils flared as he used his powerful sense of smell. His eyes snapped open.

"Blood," he said. "There was a lot of it."

My heart tripped as Milo turned toward the hallway. I followed him into Nicholas's bedroom.

I walked in behind him and nearly dropped to my knees. It was a vision. Almost an illusion. In an instant, I saw blood splattered all over the far wall and dripping down to the floor. When I blinked, the wall was clean and white.

"There," Milo said, pointing to the exact spot where I'd seen the vision.

He went to the wall and sniffed. "This was covered with blood," he said. He let his index finger turn into a single claw and scratched at the paint.

"This is new," he said. The paint beneath his scraping was light blue.

My legs shaking, I went to where Milo pointed and pressed a flat hand against the wall. Again, I saw the vision with all the blood.

"It was here," I said. "He died right here."

Milo nodded. "I smell death. Do you?"

I shook my head. "I can see flashes."

"His scent was similar to yours," he said. "Familiar, anyway. Now, what do you need?"

I ran my fingers along the wall. They'd done a good job of cleaning up the physical evidence of the violence that took place here. But something had been left behind.

I knelt near the baseboards. I pulled one away. Sure enough, I could see a dark-brown stain. Milo knelt beside me.

"Dried blood," he said. "They missed it. Whoever cleaned this up."

"It was here," I said. "They killed him here."

I wasn't psychometric. I had no extra-sensory perception through touch. I had never been prone to visions like this. And yet, if I closed my eyes, I could feel my brother's pain. His death had been quick, violent, and filled with agony.

I broke into a cold sweat and staggered backward.

"They've been lying," I said. "The coven's been lying. Nicholas was murdered."

Milo nodded. "I sense it too. Do you see anything?"

I shook my head. "No. I just feel ... him."

"What do you want to do here?" Milo asked. "I think we need to hurry up and get out of here. I was supposed to wait for backup anyway. Do you have what you need?"

It got hard to breathe. This was a spell. My brother had cast something in the seconds before he died. Every cell in my body told me he'd been trying to send a message.

"I need more time," I said. "I need ... something."

Milo stood straight up. His wolf eyes glinted and his nostrils flared. "We don't have it," he said.

"There's something wrong about this place, Nadia. I need to get you out of here. Now."

"Wait," I said as he tried to gently pull me up from my crouched position by the wall.

I reached for my backpack and pulled a locket out of the side pocket. It didn't fit me anymore, the chain was way too small. I could only wear it wrapped around my wrist now. My mother had given it to me on my fifth birthday. Inside was a picture of the four of us. Nicholas, my mom and dad, and me. I took out the fading oval image and slipped it back into the bag.

The locket itself was made of 24-karat gold. It would make the perfect container for what I had in mind.

"I need some of the blood," I said.

Milo's eyes narrowed.

"Not for here," I reassured him. "I'm not going to try casting anything here. But if this is Nicholas's blood, I might be able to conjure something that'll tell me who did this. Maybe even why."

Milo pursed his lips. I held the locket open and he guessed my mind.

Milo knelt beside me. He splayed his right hand and let his claws out. Gently, he used his index finger to scrape some of the blood off the wall. It came away like a fine brownish-red powder. He tapped it into the open locket. I closed it and clasped it against my chest.

"I hope that's enough," I said.

"Let's go," Milo said, his wolf coming out just enough to give his voice a raspy edge.

He took me by the hand. We made our way to the door.

I heard voices outside and Milo froze. He looked at me.

"Is there a back way out of here?"

Swallowing hard, I nodded. "I think so. Off the kitchen. It leads into the alley."

We changed direction. Milo was moving so fast I had to run to keep up with him. He opened the back door and started toward the alley.

I was right behind him. I had one foot on the step, the other still on the kitchen floor.

That's when it happened.

Something struck me right in the chest and took the air from my lungs. Instinct fueled me. I tried to call on the wind to push the force away.

But I had nothing. It was as if something had reached into my heart and pulled the source of my power straight out of me. I couldn't see. I couldn't breathe. The only concrete sense I had was Milo's steady heartbeat thumping inside me.

He reared back, seeing me in distress.

"Nadia?" he barked.

"Nadia!"

I couldn't answer. I was falling fast and hard.

My mind was clear but my body was no longer my own. I tried to form words. To warn Milo. It was a spell, laid so cleverly at the back door. I felt like an idiot. I'd been looking for one as we came into the house. But this one had been triggered by us leaving.

I had nothing. No words. No air. No strength. There was only Milo to pull me back from the abyss.

I felt strong arms wrap around me. He was so big, so solid, so warm. Then the ground whizzed by beneath me as Milo picked up speed and raced down the alley.

The next thing I knew, I was face down, my cheek pressed against the black leather seat in the back of the SUV. Milo's tires squealed as he pulled away from the curb.

I don't know how far we drove. I had no sense of where we were going. I faded in and out as I fought against the spell that blocked me from The Source.

Then it was dark. We'd stopped moving. I looked up and saw stars. I felt the cold air against my skin but I was warm, almost sweating.

Milo held me in his arms and slowly, achingly, I found a way to center myself. I locked eyes with Milo. His were glinting gold and filled with concern.

I drew a great, convulsive breath, then arched sideways, spitting out black smoke.

"Nadia?" Milo said.

I had control. Barely. With Milo's help, I found my way to a sitting position.

"I'm okay," I managed to say. He produced a water bottle and I took the first, slow sip.

"Another booby trap," I said. "The coven. I think they anticipated I'd go there."

"Can they track you from it?" he asked, his voice filled with alarm.

"Maybe," I said. "I don't know for sure."

I drew strength from Milo's touch. If he hadn't been

there, I would have collapsed in the alley. I had the keen sense that this wolf had just saved my life.

"Where are we?" I asked, trying to get my bearings.

"Somewhere I can keep you safe," he said. "We're not that far from Wild Lake. Northern Michigan. These are wolf shifter lands. I don't exactly have permission to be here, but no witch in their right mind would venture into these woods. They won't follow us here."

"Good," I said. But there was something in his eyes that gave me pause.

Milo had taken us somewhere my kind would never go. It dawned on me the same might be true for his people.

"Milo?" I asked. "We're completely on our own now, aren't we?"

His face darkened. He gave me a grim nod.

"For now," he said. "Until I can figure out the next move. It's just going to be you and me."

CHAPTER ELEVEN

MILO

Something was wrong. I made camp near a small stream. This was one of Wolfguard's safe haven sites. It was neutral territory between the bear shifter clans of Wild Ridge and the wolf packs of Wild Lake. A few years back, one of Payne's associates had forged an alliance with the Wild Lake wolves. They generally stayed out of Wolfguard affairs as we stayed out of theirs, but we had permission to stay here if there was an emergency.

As I watched Nadia sleep, I knew things might get worse before they got better. Her brow furrowed as she dreamt. I pressed a hand to her forehead. She felt feverish.

My heart skipped with alarm. Whatever spell she'd triggered back at her brother's did something to her. She tried to cover. She kept telling me she was all right, but I knew better. Her eyes still seemed cloudy. She'd been passed out cold the whole way from Eagle Point to these woods.

I ditched the SUV as well as my cell phone ten miles from Nicholas's apartment. I had one way left to communicate with Wolfguard. Confident that Nadia's condition was stable for now, I pulled the clunky satellite phone out of the footlocker we'd buried near the campsite.

Though I hated to venture even a few feet from Nadia, I emerged from the tent and took a seat on a fallen log near the stream. My cousin Erik answered on the first ring.

"Milo," he said, breathless. "Where the hell are you?"

"Safe," I said. "I've taken the target to a safe haven. It's better I don't tell you which one."

"What happened at Eagle Point?" he asked, his voice sharp with alarm.

"Have you seen it?" I asked.

"Milo, there's nothing left of it."

"What?" I asked.

"The whole building burned to the ground by the time we got there. Fire crews couldn't control the blaze. It was elemental magic. At first, we worried maybe you were inside. Why the hell didn't you answer your cell? Payne's losing his mind. So are we."

I ran a hand over my chin. Dammit.

"Another damn spell," I said. "Erik, this girl's coven wants her dead. She got hit with something as we were leaving. There's more to this than we were led to believe. What has Payne told you?"

Erik let out a sigh. "He said you're starting to suspect members of The Ring might be attached to this job. Milo, he wants you to abort. He's given the order. You need to come back in. Leave the girl behind if you have to."

His words stabbed through me. I knew with absolute certainty I could not leave Nadia behind.

"Erik," I said. "Listen to me. I think Nadia Bach and her brother were getting close to finding something terrible out about that coven. She thinks the coven might have been responsible for killing Nicholas Bach. They told her it was a heart condition. But we were there. In his apartment. It had been scrubbed, but it was a crime scene. Traces of blood splattered all over his bedroom wall but painted over. He didn't die of natural causes."

"Milo," Erik said. "That's none of our business. We don't interfere in witch affairs."

"We do if that coven is aligning itself with The Ring!" I shouted. Then I looked back toward the tent. Nadia hadn't stirred.

Sighing, I lowered my voice. "The Ring is dangerous to us," I said. "They tried to traffic our Uncle Val's mate. It's only been a couple of months since Leo stopped them from procuring a blood diamond they would have weaponized against us. Now they're after this witch. Every time we've come up against members of The Ring, they've been actively trying to hurt shifters, Erik. This thing with Nadia Bach has turned into something else. I have to make sure The Ring can't find her. And I have to know what the hell it is they want with her in the first place. You tell that to Payne."

"Tell him yourself," Erik said. "Get out of the field. Come in. Payne will listen to reason. It's no good for you to be out there with no backup. We don't know what we're dealing with. Let us help you, cousin!"

"No," I growled. "I'm going to keep Nadia safe. The best way to do that is by staying right where I am for now. You need to relay everything I just told you to Payne. The mission needs to change. Tell Payne I want Nadia Bach to have the full protection of Wolfguard. Every resource we can."

Erik growled into the phone. "Milo, listen to me," he said. "You're as close to me as any brother. You know our family loyalty is stronger than even what we pledged to Wolfguard. But I'm worried you're not thinking clearly. You're out in the field alone with a witch. A witch who murdered one of her own kind."

"She says it was self-defense," I said.

"So let her plead her case to her people. That's none of our business."

"She's my business," I said, my voice low and threatening. Even over the phone, I knew Erik could read my meaning though I didn't come out and say the actual words.

She was mine. Nadia was mine.

After a pause, Erik said, "Has it occurred to you that what you're feeling might not be real? This woman ... it could be a spell, Milo. You have to at least consider the possibility."

I squeezed my eyes shut and curled my fist. I wanted to smash something. As it was, I'm surprised I didn't crush the phone.

"I'm in control of myself and my wolf," I said. "Just do what I asked. Tell Payne I want to extend our protection to

Nadia. And tell him I'm doing it anyway, with or without Wolfguard behind me. Do you understand?"

Erik went silent for a moment. When he spoke again, his voice sounded hollow.

"I understand," he answered. I hung up before he could say anything else.

It was almost dawn. I left the embankment and headed back to the tent. Nadia was still in a fitful sleep. When I touched her forehead again, her fever had broken but her tee-shirt was pasted to her from sweat.

My wolf stirred as I looked at her. She had lean, long muscles, a taut stomach. I couldn't tear my eyes away from the swell of her breasts.

I wanted her.

My need for it burned through me hotter than any fever. Payne, Erik, all the others worried it was just a spell she'd cast to keep me from finishing this job.

I sat beside her and smoothed the hair away from her face. Nadia slept with her lips slightly apart, almost as if she dreamed of being kissed.

My whole body trembled with my craving for her. Oh, it was magic that drew me to her all right. But was it hers, or fate's?

She murmured something, stirred, and moved from her side to her back. The thin blanket I'd put over her dipped down, exposing her from the waist down. She slept in her underwear. A growl of desire ripped through me. I felt her heat.

I leaned in close, trying to make out what she was saying. It was nonsense, at first. I laid my head next to hers and grew bold. I traced a line over her shoulder, down her arm. I stopped just short of cupping her ass.

I wanted that. I wanted to pull her against me and feel the length of her body.

"Milo," she moaned.

"I'm here," I whispered back. She was still dead to the world. I sensed her rhythmic heartbeat. I knew with total clarity that it would beat alongside my own.

My mate. A witch.

If I claimed her, I would sense her fears. I would bind myself to her forever. I already knew how sweet she would taste.

It wasn't unprecedented. I'd heard there was a Wild Ridge bear who'd mated to a witch. But bears are one thing, wolves are different.

She was supposed to be my enemy. The wars between shifters and witches raged for thousands of years. It was part of our DNA. And yet, I didn't care anymore. I only cared that this particular witch needed my help. The instant I felt her pain, I knew I'd die before I let anything happen to her.

"What did you do to me, witch?" I whispered, winding a lock of her hair between my fingers.

There were no guarantees Erik could convince Payne to grant my request. Hell, Erik might not even want him to. This very moment, the two of them could be trying to figure out how to track me and bring me in, whether I went willingly or not.

Would I go willingly? I had to count my breaths to

steady my wolf. Would I turn my back on Wolfguard for Nadia? Would I turn my back on my family?

I prayed it wouldn't come to that. Once they heard Nadia's side of the story, they'd never force me to turn her over to her coven. Even the thought of it stirred my most primal rage.

I would kill for her. I would die for her.

Nadia's nightmare returned. She arched her back and cried out in pain. Instinct fueled me and I gathered her in my arms. Her skin was hot to the touch again.

"Nadia," I whispered. "Stay with me. You're safe here. I won't let them find you."

Her eyes fluttered open. My heart dropped. The irises had gone black again. She was looking straight at me but I knew she couldn't see me.

God.

What would I do if she didn't get better? Wolfguard had deep resources, but I didn't know how to reverse a spell if she stayed in the grips of this one.

Her eyes came back into focus. Thank God. She blinked hard then gripped my shoulders, her fingernails digging into me.

"Milo?" she gasped.

"I'm here," I said. "You're safe."

I grabbed one end of the blanket and mopped her brow. I found a water bottle and brought it to her lips.

"Drink this," I said, still cradling Nadia in my arms.

She drank slowly at first. Then, all at once, her strength seemed to come back. She sat upright and took the bottle from me, practically downing it.

She wiped her mouth with the back of her hand and met my stare.

"What happened?" she asked. "How long was I out?"

"Most of the night," I said. "You were having nightmares. I couldn't wake you up."

"I feel hungover," she said.

"The spell," I asked. "Is it still ... active?"

She considered my words. With one hand, she smoothed her hair back then wrapped her arms around herself.

"I'm okay," she said. "I think."

"What was it?"

She shook her head. "A warning, maybe. An alarm. They tried to get inside my head. I could *feel* them."

"Who?"

"I'm not sure. Maybe the coven," she answered. "I think ... I don't know what made me think to shut down. It's like I went into power-saving mode."

"Handy trick," I said. My heart was still racing with terror. I could fight an enemy I could see. One that would bleed. If the coven could attack her from within, there was only one way I knew to fight back.

Nadia's eyes met mine. For an instant, I felt as though she knew my mind. She went up on her knees and put a hand to my chest.

"Milo," she whispered. "I don't want to be alone."

"You're not," I said, my voice rising. "I won't let them get to you. Do you understand? No matter what."

Everything around us went deadly silent. All except for the racing beat of our hearts.

She knew. She felt it too.

I don't even remember who moved first. But the next thing I knew, Nadia's lips found mine. I pulled her into my arms.

I would drown in her. I would lose myself in her. And I would destroy anything that tried to take her away from me.

CHAPTER TWELVE

NADIA

Something changed. Milo's wolf eyes blazed hot. The fog lifted from my head and I became keenly aware of every inch of my body. His arm was solid beneath me. I lay across Milo's lap. Gently, he helped me up.

"How do you feel?" he asked.

A chill went through me. My fever had broken. I felt at first numb, then a flood of emotions went through me. I'd been wrong about everything. Grief slammed into my chest nearly taking my breath away all over again.

Milo moved. He had his hands on my arms.

"We need help," he said. "There's got to be a doctor. Someone who knows how to deal with your ... with ..."

I put a hand up. "No," I said. "It's not what you think."

"Nadia," he said. "You got hit with something powerful. I felt it go through you."

Just that. A simple sentence. And it changed everything.

Milo felt what I felt. I'd been drawing strength from him since the moment he first touched me. Now I knew what he'd done.

He'd tried to shield me from his conversation with his cousin and the men of Wolfguard. But I heard it all. He'd gone off-script. He'd turned his back on them. For me.

"It was Nicholas," I said. The moment the words were out of my mouth, I became absolutely sure.

"What?"

"It wasn't a booby trap like I laid for you back at the campsite," I said. "I think it was a message. That was my brother's magic. I'm sure of it."

As I got my feet back under me, I began to sort out the fevered dreams I'd had. "He knew I'd come," I said. "Nicholas counted on it. Milo, I was right about all of it. Nicholas found out something about the coven. I think they've been infiltrated by The Ring. I think that's what my brother was trying to warn me about."

My backpack leaned against the side of the tent. In it, I'd placed the locket containing my brother's dried blood. I fished it out.

"Tell me what you're going to do with that?" he asked.

I took a breath, knowing Milo was going to hate what I was about to say.

"I have to do what everyone's accused me of. It's the only way I'll be able to see who spilled Nicholas's blood."

Milo clenched his jaw. "No," he said. "It's too dangerous."

"It's dangerous," I admitted. "But not too dangerous. Not if ... if I take precautions."

Milo searched my face. I sat down slowly, drawing my knees up in the corner of the tent. It was getting cold and dark outside. But in here, the heat was rising.

He came to me.

"What precautions?" he said.

"I was his anchor," I said. "My brother. He used dark magic to set up that spell. They can't track me with it. That was the whole point, I think. It's why my entire coven hasn't come down on our heads. Nicholas cast it to help hide me from them. He's protecting me even now."

Hot tears stung my eyes. So much wasted time. I should have left the coven with Nicholas months ago. I'd been too stubborn. I'd listened to all the wrong people.

"He's gone," Milo said. "You're saying your brother used you to keep him from going over the edge. So now, you need someone to do that for you."

I looked up at him. A lump caught in my throat.

"Milo ..."

"You're mine," he whispered. "Tell me the truth. Is it a spell?"

I met his gaze. His golden eyes cut through me. My eyes had never felt more clear.

I shook my head.

"No," I said. "The only magic I've used on you was the spell that knocked you in the gut, and the cheap trick that made those plastic zip ties look like Dragonsteel for half a second. I swear it."

He threaded his fingers through my hair. "Then this is real."

This.

There were no good words to describe how I felt around him. His touch quickened my pulse. His rose along with it.

"You're mine," he declared. Desire thrummed through me.

It was impossible. A witch and a wolf. And yet, it was the truest thing I'd ever known. It had been in my heart since the day I was born.

"Yes," I whispered.

Milo let out a groan. I felt his wolf simmering so close to the surface.

"Show me," I said. At that moment, I wanted to see what was inside of him. I needed it.

Milo rose. He took me by the hand and led me out of the tent. A full moon hung high, with a golden glow shadowing it. A hunter's moon. It was perfect.

Milo slipped out of his jeans and cast them aside.

Magic.

I was brimming with it, but just then, Milo's shimmered. He dropped to all fours. With no more effort than breathing, his muscles reformed. Silvery-black fur covered him. His pointed ears tilted back. He pawed the ground and his magnificent wolf came to me.

I knelt before him, burying my fingers in his fur. He was both coarse and silky. I ran my hand down his flank then nuzzled against his neck.

He smelled like the woods. Musk and magic all his own.

This wolf. My wolf. Without words I felt him swear an oath.

Mine. You're mine.

Instinct fueled me. I slipped off my tank top and stepped out of my underwear. Milo's eyes glinted. His tail went up. He turned and raced down to the stream.

Running, I followed him. He found a patch of soft, mossy grass in the shadow of the trees. It was so dark here, Milo's wolf turned practically invisible. But I would sense him anywhere, even blindfolded.

Milo shifted. He rose. The powerful muscles of his quads flexed as he took a step toward me. He held his arms out and I went into them, pressing my naked body against his.

He was hard and warm.

"Milo," I whispered.

"You're mine, Nadia," he said, as if that answered all the questions in the world. In a sense, it did.

He hooked a finger beneath my chin and tilted my face toward his.

He was gentle as he kissed me, his arms enveloping me. Heat spread from my core, outward. I didn't want gentle. Not now.

I slid my fingers up his chest. Milo lifted me. I wrapped my legs around his waist. He flipped me, setting me down in the moss on my back. Then he spread my knees flat, exposing me to him.

From here, he would know. He could see. I throbbed for him. I arched my back, offering myself up to him.

"God," he whispered. "Nadia. You're ... everything."

"Please," I begged. I reached for him, drawing him down on me. My fingers closed gently around him. He was huge and hard as granite. I stroked him. He threw his head back and groaned.

He devoured me with kisses. First my lips, then he moved down the column of my throat. My breath hitched as he found his way between my breasts. He kneaded one, then the other with his skillful hands. He drew each of my nipples into peaks in turn. He licked them, stringing me tight as a bow. An instrument that he could play to perfection.

All I could do was spread my legs wider. Dig my fingers into the soft earth. Milo knew just how to play me. He brought me so close to the edge with the rough pads of his fingers, stroking my sensitive bud, making it pebble and pulse.

"Be still," he said, his voice a wicked whisper. "Be patient." I couldn't. I writhed and thrust my hips.

"Look at you," he said. "God. I could stare at you like this forever. You're so wet. So ready."

"Please," I pleaded.

"Soon," he promised. "There's no one here but us. We have all night."

Oh. I knew then that he'd take it. Before the sun rose again, Milo would stretch me to the ends of myself. And I would rise to it. Whatever he wanted. However he wanted. As long as he wanted. Because I wanted all of it too.

He brought me to my knees then gently guided me to all fours. He stroked me again, teasing out my swollen folds. My juices coated us both.

"So ready," he whispered. "Just look at my little witch."

A breeze lifted my hair although the trees around us stayed perfectly still. Milo had stirred my magic. I felt it uncoil and stretch.

He positioned himself behind me, stroking himself. I felt him press against my opening. I bent lower, angling my hips upward in invitation.

Then Milo gave me what my body had begged for. I gripped the earth as he entered me. So big. So wide. I opened for him, inch by inch. He filled me whole.

I saw stars. New magic swirled within me. His joined mine. Once Milo was fully embedded inside me, I lost control. So did he.

We found a punishing rhythm. Wild. Primal. Elemental magic. Leaves lifted off the ground and swirled around us.

We were in the eye of a storm. It seemed the stars themselves had become caught up in the cyclone.

He took me from behind. Then the world spun and I was on my back, facing him, my legs wrapped around his shoulders. So deep. So full. So perfect.

The storm raged. We spun with it, but never got dizzy.

Milo's fangs dropped.

"Yes!" I cried. He didn't need to say the words. I knew what this meant. I was his. Fated mates. Impossible. A witch. A wolf. But it was true.

I would have let him claim me all the way that night. I wanted it. But Milo held back just that much. I didn't.

He had me on my knees again. I tasted him. He tasted me. Over and over we came. No sooner had one wave crashed, then we started again.

Milo took me every way there was. Except for one. I felt a pulsing need at the base of my neck. I didn't know shifter law. But instinct gave me answers and showed me the truth. He was meant to bite me there. Mark me. Claim me as his mate forever.

He stopped just short, grazing his fangs along that sensitive spot, though I begged for the bite.

Finally, as the sun crested over the tree line, Milo pulled me against him. We'd coupled so many times I lost count. At least a dozen. I was spent. Sore. Exhausted. But I knew if he wanted it, I would rise to him as many more times as he wanted.

"Nadia," he whispered my name. I felt calm for the first time in weeks. Content. Safe. Protected and loved.

Early spring, and it was still near freezing in the morning. I didn't feel the cold. Milo warmed me. He carried me to the stream and we bathed each other. Then we walked hand in hand back to the tent.

I was starving. My bones felt like they'd turned to rubber. In spite of all that, I felt the faintest pulse of need once more.

We lay beside each other, stretched out and face to face. Milo's eyes filled with tenderness as he raked them over my body. We'd grown as familiar as a couple who'd spent years together. He traced circles around my nipples then brought them to his mouth.

"You're incredible," he whispered.

I blushed for the first time. "That was ... I mean ... what was that?"

Milo smiled and went up on one elbow. "I told you," he said. "Nadia, you're mine."

Without thinking, I put a hand to the back of my neck. I still felt a craving there.

"I wanted you to bite me," I said.

Milo's eyes darkened with lust. He shifted, bringing himself into a sitting position. He ran a hand through his hair.

"About that," he said. "There are things I should have told you before we ..."

I sat up with him.

"Milo," I said, touching his face. "I'm not afraid."

His gaze dropped. He took my hand in his. "After I tell you everything," he said, "I think you might be."

CHAPTER THIRTEEN

MILO

I thought I knew what magic was. I thought I understood the ends of my own. I'd only ever scratched the surface.

Everything was different now. Even the air in my lungs. Nadia's magic enveloped me. She was the storm and the calm at the center of my heart.

She looked at me, her heart beating in time with mine. She had questions. I owed her answers. I had been so close to branding her with my Alpha's mark. How I found the strength to hold back, I didn't know. But as much as destiny drew me to her, she had to understand what it all meant with her eyes wide open. Instinct wasn't enough for this.

She rubbed a hand across the base of her neck. I didn't even have to tell her. Her body knew that's where I'd mark her as mine.

"Why did you stop?" she asked.

"Because I don't think you're ready for it," I said.

Her brow furrowed. "I'm not ... inexperienced, Milo." she said. Jealousy flared, making my vision brighten. I knew she could see my wolf eyes glint. I took a breath to get a handle on it.

No one. No man would touch her again if I had anything to say about it.

"You are about this," I said. I reached for her, putting my hand over hers at the base of her neck.

"You feel me," I said. "In here." I put my free hand over her heart.

"Yes."

"When I mark you, it will grow stronger. And I'll want to do it again and again. In time, you'll be able to hear my thoughts. And I'll hear yours. If you're scared or hurt, I'll know it. I'll come to you. This feeling ... lust ... it's just the beginning, Nadia."

She blushed. "I know. I mean ... even now. After ... er ... the whole night. I still want you."

Desire warmed me. I'd have given just about anything to stay there in the woods with her, rutting like wild animals for days. It would be too easy to forget what brought us together in the first place. I'd bought us some time for now, but only a little.

"I want you too," I said. "I thought it was something you were doing at first. A spell. Now I know it's not."

"Milo," she said. "I haven't lied to you. Not once."

My heart fell. She didn't say it, but the truth was there between us. I couldn't say the same. I lied to her when we first met about who I was and what I wanted from her.

"I know," I said. "And I'm sorry I can't say the same. I can now though."

"What about Wolfguard?" she asked. "They won't stop coming for me. Neither will my coven."

She reached into her pack and pulled out the locket with her brother's blood in it.

"What are you going to do with that?" I asked.

"I need you to trust me," she said. "I can use magic. I told you about a spell. If it works, I can see his last moments. I'll be able to tell who and what killed him."

My wolf stirred. It felt like that baser part of me understood something on an instinctual level I hadn't yet caught up with logically. It could only mean one thing.

"Dark magic," I said. "Nadia, it's a risk."

She nodded.

"What happens if you can't control it?"

She reached for me. "You have to believe me that I can. Especially with you here. You can anchor me."

I didn't like it one bit. "Then what?" I said.

"If I can prove what Nicholas tried to, that members of our coven have sold us out to The Ring, I can hold the people who hurt him accountable. I can bring my brother's killer to justice."

This was insanity. I felt what her brother's last spell did to her. Whether it was light or dark, it hurt her. Every instinct in me told me her coven wouldn't give up its secrets that easily.

"I can't fully protect you out here," I said, hating to admit it even to myself. "I need backup. I need to bring you in."

Nadia recoiled. Terror filled her eyes and it echoed through me. I put my hands on her shoulders.

"I meant what I said. Even without my mark, you're my mate, Nadia. You have my protection. I swear it."

"Your firm wants to sell me to the coven. The coven wants to turn me over to The Ring."

I sighed. "My firm doesn't know the full story. You need to let me tell it. The men I work for, they've seen how dangerous The Ring is. Just last year, my uncle kept his mate from being trafficked by them. My cousin stopped a Ring-backed plot to steal a powerful gemstone. We know what they're capable of."

"Then you know they're getting bolder," Nadia said. "I don't know what their endgame is, but I know it's bad. They're pitting shifters and witches against each other again. Why do you think that is?"

I grimaced. I didn't have an answer for her. But the more time we wasted, the worse it was going to get.

"Payne Fallon," I said. "You have to know what kind of man he is."

Nadia blinked. "I know he's being paid by my coven."

"He started Wolfguard Security. You remember I told you he was part of the resistance that overthrew a *Tyrannous Alpha* who controlled the Kentucky shifters. We have information that leads us to believe The Ring backed that monster. So, their interest is destabilizing shifter groups. And if what you're saying is true, then they're going after covens too. Probably for the same reason."

"Why?" she asked. "It doesn't make sense."

"The only thing they'd have to gain by that kind of

chaos is control. They pit their enemies against each other. Witches and shifters. Shifters and shifters. I don't know. Maybe both."

Nadia shook her head. "But for all we know, shifters and witches *are* part of The Ring. Those men at the gas station had borrowed power. It came from somewhere."

"Nadia," I said. "I trust Payne Fallon. And I trust the Kalenkovs, my family. You? You're part of it now. They need to know you're my mate. The oath I just swore extends to them as well."

Her heart fluttered with uncertainty. I couldn't blame her. This was all new to her. It was new to me too. But I would bet my life I'd have the loyalty of my family and my firm.

"Let me check in," I said. "We're vulnerable out here. I can better protect you from the Detroit field office or back in Chicago. Then, if you need to perform your spell, I'll back you."

"Milo ..."

"Trust me," I said. I drew her to me and kissed her forehead.

My satellite phone buzzed in the corner of the tent. I was at least an hour past my appointed check-in time. If I didn't call back, Payne would try to send reinforcements and it would be harder for me to control it.

"I need to take that," I said. "Just wait here. I'll know if anything bigger than a chipmunk comes near you, Nadia."

She smiled and kissed me back. I picked up the phone and headed out of the tent and back downstream.

"It's Milo," I answered.

"Milo, where the hell have you been?" Erik demanded. "You don't get to go radio silent on this one."

"Erik," I said. "The situation has changed. I need you to listen to me."

"I am," he spat.

"Nadia Bach ... she's ... she's under my protection. Which means she's under yours."

"What?"

Above me, a bald eagle took flight from the top of a pine tree. She made a majestic arc and swooped down further upstream.

"Erik," I said. "Nadia's my fated mate."

Erik fell silent except for his breathing.

"Cousin?" I said.

"I'm listening," he said.

"That's all there is to it. She's mine."

"How can you be sure?" he asked.

This got a laugh out of me. "Spoken like a man who hasn't found his yet. Trust me, your time will come. When it does, you'll know why that's a ridiculous question to ask. I know because I know. Talk to Val and Leo. To my father. Hell, even Grace and Gideon could clue you in."

My sister Grace mated with a dragon-shifter last year. It was a secret we'd been sworn to keep. Most of the rest of the world believed dragons were still extinct.

"Milo," Erik said. "You don't know everything there is to know about Nadia Bach. Payne had a meeting with the leader of her coven last night. The man who hired us in the first place. He had some disturbing new details about her."

My heart stopped cold. "What details?"

"Nadia Bach is a cold-blooded killer," Erik said. "She's been lying to you. This man she killed? From her coven? It wasn't self-defense. Milo, he was an old man. Crippled. And he was unconscious in a hospital bed when she ... God. I can't even describe what she did. But I don't have to. There was security footage. Payne's given me permission to send it to you. You need to see it. And you need to be very careful around her."

The air left my lungs in a whoosh. Nothing Erik said made sense.

"I'm sending it now," he said. "Videotext. Look at it. I'll wait on the line."

It was as if someone else had taken over my body. I pulled the phone away and waited for Erik's video to download.

I sank down and sat on a flat rock by the stream. I pressed the play button.

The scene was as Erik described. A skinny, elderly man lay in a hospital bed. His eyes were vacant, sightless, and he was hooked up to a million tubes.

Then a shadow fell over his face. Nadia appeared. She was crying at first, but she stood strong and tall at the foot of his bed. The man never even seemed to know she was there.

Then a storm raged inside the room. His blankets flapped aside, revealing old, gnarled legs. Nadia's eyes glinted blue then went purest black. Her hair blew straight up. The old man lifted off the bed. He arched his back as Nadia raised her hands. She pointed them at him.

He hung in mid-air, limp, blind, immobile. Then his

whole body crumpled. There was no sound in the video, but I watched as every bone in his body seemed to break, one by one, contorting at wrong angles.

He woke then at the very last second, his face a mask of agony. Nadia was done with him. He dropped to the ground and blood poured out of his eyes and mouth. Nadia turned. When she walked out of the room, I saw her face full-on. She was smiling.

"Milo?

Erik's voice finally reached me.

"I'm here," I said.

"Milo, do you see now? She's dangerous. Deadly. And I think she might have cast a spell to make you think she's your fated mate. Cousin, it might not be real. You have to bring her in. Do you hear me? Tell me where you are. We can send a team within the hour."

I couldn't think straight. This had to be a trick. A lie. Nadia swore the man she killed had tried to hurt her, to steal her magic.

Had it all been lies? A sick thought crept in my heart. What if she'd lied about her brother as well? What if Nadia herself had been the one to kill him? The bloodstains in his room were eerily similar to what she'd done in the video to the old man.

No. It couldn't be a trick. I didn't know if I could trust my mind or my heart.

"Milo?"

"I'm here," I said, turning back toward the camp. Nadia emerged from the tent, beautiful, glowing. Her eyes filled with joy as she spotted me and waved.

"I've got it under control," I said. "I'll bring her in myself. She trusts me. Tell Payne to expect us at the Detroit field office by morning."

I clicked off the call and slid the phone in my pocket as I walked upstream to meet Nadia.

CHAPTER FOURTEEN

Nadia

Milo hadn't come back yet. My stomach growled and I rustled through the supplies he brought, finding some jerky and some tin-foil-wrapped toaster pastries. He kept some bottled water stacked in the corner. I grabbed one and made my way out of the tent.

The locket with Nicholas's blood hung around my wrist. Moonlight cast it in shadows. No moon would be ideal, but I knew I could make it work.

I pulled the tattered book page out of my pocket and laid it flat on the grass. It was the one thing I'd stolen from the coven before I left. A single page from one of the oldest grimoires we had left. Pure dark magic.

I said the incantation in my head, not daring to speak it out loud yet. It called for no ingredients but an open sky and a drop of blood. I hoped what I had would be enough. It didn't say the blood had to be fresh or wet.

I sat with my back against the tree, letting the breeze wash over me. It gave me strength. Centered me. The usual outdoor noises fell away and I was left with the faint pulse of my own heartbeat. Then there was Milo's beneath that.

My fated mate. I could still feel his touch lingering on every part of me. A new craving burned through me. It was as if I drew as much strength from him as I did from the wind. I hugged myself, feeling the most content I had since the moment I started getting strange texts from my brother. For the first time in all the months since I lost him, that grief felt manageable. It still burned, but I could see a future where I could put it in a compartment in my heart and live around it.

But the worst was yet to come. Milo said he trusted me. He'd asked me to trust him. I had no idea how bad things might get tonight when I tried to cast this spell. And I hadn't yet told him what I planned to do depending on what it revealed. If I could clearly see who killed my brother, I knew I had to make him or her pay.

It was chilly here in the shade. It was still a good six weeks before summer came. Northern Michigan might freeze every night for weeks. The Midwest didn't feel like home anymore after what happened with the coven. I didn't know where that was anymore.

No.

The moment the thought entered my mind, I knew that wasn't entirely true. Milo was home. Or he could be if I let him.

A shadow crossed in front of me. My heart warmed as

Milo came through the trees. His look was solemn, but his eyes sparked as they met mine.

He stood stock-still for a moment, considering me. My heart skipped as I realized in an instant he was trying to modulate his heartbeat. Something was wrong.

"Come sit with me," I said.

A muscle twitched near his jaw. He hesitated for a moment, then he walked up the slight hill and took a seat beside me, leaning against the oak tree like I did.

"Something's wrong," I said. "I can sense it. I can't tell anymore if that's witch magic, or something shifter."

"It has to be both," he said. "I think our magic is interlaced now. Or ... it wants to be."

"Tell me what it is," I said, not sure if I really wanted the answers I sought. Just then, I had a vision. More of a dream, really. A wish. I considered the best way to articulate it. Then decided not to care.

"What if we don't go back?" I said.

His eyes narrowed as he turned to me.

"What do you mean?"

"You spoke to your boss, didn't you? That's what that look in your eyes means. They still think I'm some kind of dark, evil witch monster. They want the bounty on my head."

"It's not that simple," he answered, and I realized he was lying.

"So," I said. "What if we don't go back?"

"When you say that," he said. "I'm not sure you get what you're asking. You want me to turn my back on Wolfguard? On my family?"

"I do if they want you to hurt me," I said, my voice rising.

Milo flinched. He shifted, putting his hands on my arms. His skin felt so warm. My desire rose and for a moment it was hard to think past it.

"I'm not going to hurt you," he said.

"Did you tell them?" I asked. "Do they know what we are to each other?"

His eyes flickered and I knew the truth. The urge to get up and run, throw a storm between us rose up in me. Milo didn't let me go.

"Then you've made promises you can't keep," I said. "You said if you claimed me, that I'd be part of the Kalenkov family and they'd have to protect me too. So, you told them, and they won't honor it, is that it?"

He looked physically pained by my words. My instinct was to say the hell with it all and throw myself at him. His pain started to feel like my pain. He'd been so worried about me using some kind of spell on him to cloud his mind, I was beginning to think the real danger was the other way around.

"They have questions," he said. "And now so do I. But nothing's changed about what you are to me."

"What questions?"

"They showed me some security footage. Of you."

He pulled a clunky black phone out of his pocket. His fingers lingered over the screen.

"Nadia," he said. "Tell me more about the man you killed."

I brought my knees up to my chest. Suddenly, it felt cold again.

"Michael Tolliver," I said. "Like I said, he'd been a mentor to me. He was one of my father's best friends. Right after my parents died, I lived with him and his wife Shelly for a little while."

I smoothed a hair away from my face.

"He's the one who told me Nicholas died. He showed me the autopsy report. I trusted him."

"But that changed," Milo said.

"Yes, that changed. But not soon enough. Michael wasn't well. He had end-stage lung cancer. So I knew I was about to lose the only other person I was close to in the coven."

"But you said you were starting to suspect that wasn't a natural disease?"

"I started to question everything I'd been told, Milo. But I believed Michael was the one person I had left who had my best interests at heart. That changed."

His face remained unreadable, only his steady pulse belied his warring emotions. It was unsettling and familiar all at the same time.

"I'm listening," he said.

"I went to see Michael one last time at this rehab facility he was staying at. Kind of like hospice care. He wasn't expected to live much longer. He called me and told me he had a letter for me from my brother. That it was found among his personal effects. I thought that was strange because Nicholas's landlord had everything shipped to me in a box. There wasn't much.

And like I said before, I was starting to get suspicious that the coven was trying to bring me in for an inquiry. I was scared. But I had to hear what Michael had to say."

"What happened when you got there?" Milo asked.

I hugged my knees even tighter to my body. "When I got there, Michael wasn't in bed. He was standing at the window. I told him ... I told him I didn't believe what they were saying about how Nicholas died. Michael was shocked by that. He seemed pained, actually. I told him my brother had been sending these cryptic warnings for months. I wanted Michael to know I planned to pursue it. I knew the coven wasn't on board. And I knew they were going to block me."

"Then what happened?" Milo said. I had a tingling feeling at the base of my spine. This was starting to feel like a cross-examination.

"Michael was a fire mage," I said. "He hit me with something. It was like a blue bolt of lightning. His eyes were wrong. It paralyzed me for a second. It's hard to describe, but for an instant, I felt hollowed out. Like Michael ... or someone ... was trying to peel apart my soul. There was someone else in that room that day. Someone I couldn't see. Milo, I'm telling you. They were trying to kill me. Michael said something about how I should have learned to stop asking so many questions. He was having a conversation with someone who wasn't there. I think other members of the coven were tapped in. Anyway, I can't even tell you what it was I threw at him. I just acted on pure adrenaline and instinct. They probably told your firm it was dark magic I used that day. It wasn't. It felt like it was part of me. Breathless."

"Breathless?" he asked.

I nodded. "Every witch has one sort of doomsday self-defense mode. We can draw on our basic element if we have to. Mine is wind. So I took Michael's."

"Breathless," he said. "You took his literal breath away from him?"

I let my knees drop. "Yes," I said. "I didn't go there to kill him. Not even to hurt him. I trusted him. I think Nicholas did too. And I think my brother was afraid to tell me to watch out for Michael. Maybe he thought I was safer if I was ignorant. I don't know. But I swear to you, if I hadn't thrown that spell, Michael would have killed me. He used his own element. That blue lightning was meant to char me to the bone."

Milo shuddered, feeding off my own fear. He still held the phone in his hand.

"What is it?" I asked. He was holding back.

"Nadia," he said. "I told you they sent me security footage. This is what I saw."

He swiped the phone screen and handed it to me. Grainy footage from Michael's hospice room came up. He was lying, immobile on his bed. I saw myself ... or what looked like me ... walk in. But it was all wrong. Michael and I had a conversation that lasted a few minutes. For most of it, he'd been standing at the window.

None of that showed on this recording. Instead, I saw the last bit. I threw my breathless spell. Michael contorted.

His bones cracked. He bled. Then he lay on the floor motionless.

"Milo," I whispered. "This is wrong."

"What are you saying?"

I handed the phone back to him as if it had gone radioactive.

"That's not me," I said. "I mean, it looks like me. But that is *not* what happened in that room. I swear. He wasn't lying on that bed like that. He was on his feet. At the window. Just like I said."

I felt the torture inside of Milo.

"They did something to it," I said. "Doctored it."

"Wolfguard ran it through high-tech analysis," he said. "It's unaltered."

I shook my head. It felt like my own breath had left me.

"No," I said.

Instinct took over. I went to my knees in front of him. "So mark me," I said. "You said you could read my mind if you did."

"No," he said. "I said eventually we could hear each other's thoughts. Speak to each other without words. It's not the same thing as mind reading."

"Whatever," I said. "I'm telling you the truth!"

I took his hand and pressed it to my heart. Even then, I felt his lust rise along with my own.

"I'm not a cold-blooded murderer, Milo. I killed Michael because he gave me no choice. That footage is wrong. If it's not doctored then the coven did something else. They staged some kind of illusion."

"Can they do that?" he asked. "Is that a spell?"

I froze. "I don't know. Not one that I'm familiar with. But I'm not omnipotent, Milo. And I just told you. I had the sense someone else was in that room. Maybe he or she cast an illusion spell and the camera picked it up. I think I was set up. You have to believe me. You know who I am. You know what I am to you. That tape is a lie. I've told you the truth. You asked me to trust you. Now you have to trust me. For real."

He gathered my hands in his. "I want to."

"Then do it."

I realized the source of his conflict. His firm had sent him that tape to discredit me. They were siding with the coven against me.

I pulled my hands away from him. "You're supposed to bring me in."

He swallowed hard. "Nadia, you have to give me some time to ..."

"No," I said. "I am telling you my brother was murdered."

"No one's disputing that now," he said. The truth slammed down over my heart like a drawbridge.

"Oh God," I said. I saw that security footage in my mind again. "They're telling you I did it. That I killed my brother too?"

"Yes," he said. I supposed I should have been grateful he was at least being honest with me now.

"Then we need to leave," I said. "Now. We need to get as far away as we can from my coven and your firm. Until I can figure out how to fix this. Let me do this spell. Milo, you'll see what I see."

"Nadia, I'm afraid for you," he said. "Your coven knows you think your brother was killed. Don't you think performing this spell will play right into their hands? What if they're preparing for it? What if there's some way they can ... can they track you through it? It's dark magic, but are you going to stand there and tell me you won't have to connect to The Source in order to perform it?"

I pulled away from him. I felt so close to the truth and yet a thousand miles away from it. Now the coven had found a way to use Milo to stop me.

"No," I said. "It's worth the risk. I can handle myself. If you're there with me, I can handle it. You said you have a sister. If it was you. If this was about her. Can you really stand there and tell me you wouldn't try everything within your power to avenge her?"

I saw the truth in his eyes. But I still saw the fear and the doubt. I only hoped it wasn't too late to do what needed to be done.

CHAPTER FIFTEEN

MILO

Her dark eyes drew me in. Her magic was part of me. Maybe it always had been. Maybe everything Payne and the others warned me about was true. She could be lying.

This is why my kind hated witches. Nothing was ever as it seemed. Tricks. Illusions. Borrowing or stealing from wind, rain, fire, earth, and making you see things that weren't real.

But she was real. She was standing right in front of me. Tiny beads of sweat dotted her brow. My eyes traveled down the slope of her shoulder, settled on her hands. She held them folded in front of her. A neutral stance. She made herself vulnerable for me.

"Milo," she said. "I'm telling you the truth. I'm not a murderer. Not the way they're trying to make you believe."

I held the sat phone in my hand. The video froze. The play button obscured the grisly scene.

"Michael was going to kill me," she said. "He lied to me about my brother. He knew what really happened and was trying to keep me from looking deeper. That's what this whole thing has been about. They want to silence me. If my coven is in bed with The Ring, if word gets out about that, other covens won't stand for it. Witches police their own."

"Except for you," I said.

"Exactly," she said. "If I were the problem, they would have reached out to coven allies. Other witches. They didn't do that because they didn't want to risk me getting proof of what they did to Nicholas. Once I have that ... Milo, they can't hide. My coven will be broken up. They contracted Wolfguard to buy your silence."

She made sense. And yet, I couldn't discount what I saw on that video. Was it really a trick? Another spell?

I growled. "God, I hate witches," I said.

Nadia stepped back, but set her jaw into a hard line.

"And I've always hated shifters. But we're different. You're the one who made me believe that. If you turn me in. If the coven gets a hold of me ... Milo, they won't just kill me. They'll try to strip me of my power first. I won't die quickly. It'll be slow. Maddening agony you can't imagine."

Except I could. I knew in my heart I would feel every ounce of pain Nadia did. Forever. And my wolf would never let me stand aside and let it happen.

I knew it didn't matter if I believed her. Damn my soul to hell if that's what this was, but I had no choice when it came to this woman.

"How long do we have?" she asked, taking a step away from me.

It was in me to lie. I could have told her Payne and Erik gave me discretion. Of course they'd understand if she were truly my fated mate.

But I couldn't.

"I'm supposed to bring you to the Detroit field office by this evening."

She swallowed hard, her eyes searching my face.

I went to her, threading my hands through her hair. "They'll find us here if we stay."

"Milo ..."

My heart ripped in two. It seemed there was no way I could stay loyal to Wolfguard and serve my mate at the same time. The choice was mine and I had to make it now.

My lips found hers. Words couldn't sway me. The feel of her could. Nadia's touch made everything clear. Simple. Even if it meant I'd just signed my own death warrant.

"I know a place," I said as we came up for air. "It's not far. It's a risk because we'll technically be on Wild Lake lands."

"I just need a little bit of time," she said. "If you keep watch, I can do this spell." She lifted the locket from her chest.

"Milo," she said. "It'll work. I'll be able to see what happened to my brother. Who was there. Michael was covering for someone."

"But then it'll be your word against theirs?" I said.

"No," she said, the word coming out almost like a gasp. "Not with the way I have to do this. Milo, this spell will attach to my brother's killer. It'll leave a stain on him or her. It won't last forever, but if I can get word to the other covens, the killer won't be able to hide. His guilt will literally be written all over him."

I tried to process what she said. I didn't have to be a witch to know she was talking about some seriously dark magic.

"And what will it do to you?" I asked.

She took my hands. "It'll be okay. I'm strong as hell, Milo. That's what my coven has always been afraid of. That's why Nicholas didn't trust me with whatever he knew at first. And this is the only way to get out from under this. Milo ... I love you."

She stepped back, almost to give her words some room. They struck me right in the heart. I loved her too. Even if it damned us both, I loved her.

I kissed her again.

"We need to go now," I said. "And we have to leave everything behind. How fast can you move?"

She bit her lip. "With magic? Faster than you."

"No," I said sharply. Instinct told me the more she relied on magic, the easier it would be for her coven to find her.

"We'll use *my* magic this time," I said. Nadia took my hand. I could move faster in my wolf. But I was still superhuman on two legs. I scooped Nadia into my arms. My heart tripped as desire ripped through me. I needed her again. Badly. I pushed those thoughts aside as I picked up speed. The trees whizzed by in a blur.

WE REACHED the Wild Lake borderlands by nightfall. Nadia said it was perfect. A waxing moon rose. By now, Wolfguard and the Kalenkovs would know I was AWOL. There was a good chance that even if Nadia was successful, I'd be out of a job by morning.

It didn't matter. Nadia was my world now.

She moved as if she belonged here. She gave off a bluish luminescence in the light of the moon. She chose the woods again. Just a few yards ahead of us, Wild Lake itself shimmered.

"What will you need?" I asked. It was almost midnight. Nadia had found a spot in the clearing, a natural circle formed in the center of a ring of trees. It was almost as if this place had called to her. To us. I began to wonder if it had.

She sat cross-legged. She'd gathered her hair and tied it back with a strip of leather. She was barefoot, wearing a pair of jeans and a tank top. It would get down to near freezing tonight, but Nadia's skin glowed warmly. I'd given her my heat. I hadn't thought we could take the time for it. But once we got safely away from the campsite, neither of us could deny our primal need.

I'd taken her quickly. Fully. She'd gone to all fours, her back arched. Again, she'd offered me her neck.

It was even harder this time to hold back. Maybe I shouldn't have. As much as I wanted that final claiming, there was too much unsettled. If I turned my back on Wolfguard and the Kalenkovs, I didn't know how I'd provide for us. And she was outcast from her coven. I wanted to mate with her from a position of strength, not desperation.

"I just need the air," she said, reaching me. "And you."

"What's going to happen?" I asked.

She bit her lip. "Well, I've never actually done this before so your guess is as good as mine. I need you to make me a promise. No matter what happens. What you see. What you hear. Don't try to stop it. This could ... hurt."

My heart stirred. "What do you mean hurt?"

"Well," she said. "I'm not *of* the dark Source, despite what everyone wants you to think. I'm taking power from a place I'm not supposed to be. It will resist. Probably. But I don't need very much. Just a touch. In and out."

I growled. I hated everything about this. Only I had no better plan. If I could solve all of this by smashing and tearing something to bits, I would have.

"It's almost time," she said, looking up at the moon.

"Midnight," I said.

She nodded. "We've got about a minute."

She opened her locket. The air shifted. I scented the wind. There was some wildlife deeper in the woods and in and around the lake. We were miles out from any of the Wild Lake wolves' lands. I could sense those shifters in the distance and knew they could sense me. But I'd left a wide enough perimeter they wouldn't perceive me as a threat. I hoped.

"Where do you want me?" I asked.

Nadia furrowed her brow. "You know, I'm not exactly sure. Just ... stay outside the circle, but not too far outside it. Maybe get in front of me. I think it'll help if I can see you. Though ... in a sec here, things are going to start falling away."

I moved in front of her. I stood with my hands folded. I had a tree at my back. I squatted down so I was eye level with Nadia. I had the urge to shift.

"Don't!" she said, sensing my mood. "I mean ... if you can't help it later, I get it. I just think you're better off staying away from your wild side for this."

"Got it," I said.

The wind lifted her hair. The trees around us stayed still.

"Okay," she said. She tore the locket off her wrist and held it flat in her palm.

My pulse quickened. I caught a whiff of ozone. Storm clouds moved in and the sky went even blacker.

Midnight.

Nadia started chanting something. I couldn't tell if it was Latin or something even older. She rocked back and forth, still cross-legged. Static electricity made her hair stand up. After a few seconds, she went somewhere else. The chain from the locket slowly rose in the air.

My wolf growled. I dug my fingers into the ground trying to keep him under wraps. I didn't sense Nadia in any pain, but I could feel her slipping away a little.

Then the storm clouds churned. Nadia's hair lifted straight up. She began to levitate a few inches off the ground. My spine cracked. My claws came out.

She wasn't in pain. But I felt something heavy wrap its tentacles around her. Black smoke rolled in. It had a jarring sound, metal on metal.

Nadia's eyes snapped open and the whites disappeared. All that was left were two black orbs, churning like smoke.

The locket disintegrated leaving red powder behind. Nicholas's blood. It swirled in front of her. Rose up, then began to take a different shape.

I couldn't make it out. I saw figures in the red powder. A man. Another man standing in front of him.

Nadia's eyes went from black to blood red. She screamed.

I let out a howl. I was half-man, half-wolf. I felt Nadia's pain. It was as if she were being ripped apart. Something strong tried to pull her away from me.

The dark Source. I knew it by instinct. "No!" I shouted.

I stepped into the circle.

Nadia screamed again. She was on her feet. She went rigid, her back bowing at a cruel angle. I thought I heard her bones crack.

She was going. Getting smaller. It was as if the ground opened up. A gaping mouth to hell.

"Nadia!" I shouted. I lunged for her. I caught a lock of her hair. She was crying blood.

"No!"

She drew her hands back. Black smoke shot out from her fingertips. She pushed me back with it. It was as if a cannonball struck me in the chest. I fell backward and hit the base of an oak tree. I tried to scramble up.

That's when she took the air from my lungs.

Breathless.

I tried to draw air. My lungs collapsed. My head swirled.

Pain. Agony. Chaos.

Then there were lights all around.

A dozen pairs of wolf eyes forming a circle. With Nadia at the center.

I still couldn't breathe. I struggled to stay conscious.

Nadia's eyes changed, settling into their natural sable. Her hair fell gently around her shoulders. She was here. She was back. Only I was dying right in front of her.

She had blood on her hands. Her brother's blood. Whatever she'd done had made it fresh again somehow. She looked so sad.

"Don't move!"

The voice came sharp and deep. I knew it. It couldn't be. I had to be imagining it.

Nadia was surrounded. Payne, Erik, Edward, and a dozen other operatives from Wolfguard closed in. Some were shifted into their wolves, some weren't.

"No," I tried to shout. No air. No time.

Nadia took a staggering step backward and met my eyes. Hers registered with the shock of betrayal.

"No," I tried to whisper.

"Don't take another step," Erik shouted. "We won't hurt you."

Nadia threw out another blast of air that knocked Erik and a few of the others back.

The storm clouds rolled back in. I tried to reach for her. But Nadia vanished into thin air.

My breath came back in a whoosh.

CHAPTER SIXTEEN

Nadia

I felt concrete beneath my cheek rather than grass. The smells were all wrong. Dank. Mildew. Not open air.

Slowly, I opened my eyes. It was a dark, small room. I heard the torturous drip of water off a rusted drain pipe above my head.

Carefully, I raised myself to a seated position. I felt bound, but there were no ties or ropes on me anywhere.

Then everything came at me in a rush. Shifters. Lights. Milo betrayed me. My heart stung. I'd believed all of it. So stupid. He said he didn't want to mark me while everything was in turmoil with my coven and his family. Now I knew that wasn't it. He must have known by strengthening the telepathic bond between us I would have been able to sense his lies.

"So clever," I whispered. Was he in the building somewhere? I closed my eyes and tried to slow my breathing.

But I got no sense of him. God. Maybe that had all been a lie too. Were we really fated mates at all?

My eyes began to adjust to the light. There was something sticky on my hands. I smelled blood but felt no pain.

Then fragments of my memory started to come back. It wasn't my blood. It was my brother's. The spell.

I pressed my back against the concrete wall. I let my mind settle. What had I seen?

Nicholas's face wavered in my field of vision. He was smiling. He sat on the edge of his bed in the apartment in Eagle Point. He was talking to someone.

He wasn't scared. He was laughing.

Then a light shone in his eyes. A reflection off a metal blade. A knife.

Nicholas was still in his room. He was pacing, humming something.

I saw Michael standing in the corner. He was angry. Nicholas ignored him. I wanted to shout a warning. I should have known. But Michael couldn't be there. He was in a near coma in hospice care. This was a trick. The spell had gone wrong somehow.

Then Nicholas turned. He looked right at me. His smile faltered. There was blood everywhere. It splattered on the wall of his bedroom but I saw no wound on my brother. He drew the knife slowly across his wrist. Turning, he cast a spell, blowing over his wrist. The blood splattered. I saw it over and over. In reverse. In slow motion. Freeze frame.

There had been no one else in the room with my brother. The blood was his, but he didn't die. He used dark magic to multiply it somehow. Then he blew across the blade and made it disappear. Nicholas stood in front of me, his face frozen. His skin shimmered with a reddish glow.

It was the spell. It *had* worked. The stain settled on my brother. It was his magic all along.

My stomach turned as the concrete reappeared beneath me. I shook my head trying to clear it. I heard slow clapping. Then the shadows moved and my brother stepped in to view.

My heart split in two. It was Nicholas, but not. He looked at me with cold, hateful eyes.

"Welcome back," he said.

I crawled backward, bringing my knees up.

"What's going on?" I asked. "You're not real."

"Oh, I'm real," he said. He reached up and pulled a thin white string, turning on an overhead light. I squinted, adjusting to the brightness.

This was a basement with cinder block windows. I was huddled in a corner. Nicholas had a stairwell at his back. He sat down on a long wooden bench in front of me.

"You?" I said, trying to sort out the spell from reality.

No. No. No. My brother was dead. He'd been about to expose corruption in the coven.

I scrambled to my feet. Nicholas stayed seated. I moved along the wall. He just watched me with amusement.

"I don't get it," I said.

"You do," he said. "And you performed better than I could have hoped. My friends are impressed. Aren't you?"

He called up the stairs. Heavy footsteps shook the ground as two suited men descended the steps. I recognized them. They were the ones from the gas station. They'd been sent by The Ring.

My heart raced with alarm. "Michael," I said.

"Old guy had more fight in him than I realized," he said. "He was right to try to keep you from finding me. He underestimated you. Thanks for taking care of him for me."

I shook my head. "Michael was trying to protect me. From you?"

Fragments of memory seeped in. I'd sensed a presence in the room with Michael the day he tried to kill me. Nicholas. It had always been Nicholas. He was there too. He'd cloaked himself somehow. Michael hadn't tried to kill me at all. He'd been trying to kill Nicholas to save me. Oh God. And I'd killed him for it!

Nicholas shrugged. "It doesn't matter anymore. You're here. You passed the test."

"What test?" I looked from my brother to the two silent men.

"She'll do," the bald one said. "She's drawn to the darker Source. We can work with that."

"Nicholas," I said. "Tell me what's going on?"

He slapped one knee. "We're moving up in the world. The Ring has been looking to partner with the Bach family for a few generations now. I guess our Uncle Cyrus turned them down flat a few years ago. They made good on their promise to cause trouble for him. Cy figured he'd do better going rogue. So, that worked out to our advantage."

"What does The Ring want with us?" I asked.

"That's not really something you need to worry about," the bald one said. "Your coven doesn't appreciate your talents. We do. And your brother is right. We've been looking to ally with a dark wind mage for a while. Nicholas is strong, you're stronger. We're glad to have you aboard."

Nicholas rose. "So we're done here?" he asked.

"Is she ... secure?" the taller man asked.

Nicholas looked back at me. "Come here, Nadia," he said. "You don't have to be scared. Step out of the shadows so they can get a good look at you."

I don't know why I did. I judged the distance between me and the stairs. These two men weren't powerful. They were human. And no matter what else was going on, Nicholas was my brother. The borrowed power they had at the gas station had worn off.

I straightened my back. I drew in a breath and tried to cast it outward. It was just a little spell. I could knock two humans on their rears easily.

The moment I tried to tap into The Source, it bit back.

It was Nicholas. Somehow, he'd found a way to use my own power against me. They'd done something. That had to be the answer. Everything that had happened over the last year replayed in my mind.

Nicholas withdrew. Michael and other members of the coven came to me, expressing concern. I'd covered for him. He was the only family I had left. Had I been that blind to it this whole time? I saw the vision from my blood spell replay. I saw Nicholas casting a spell and throwing his own blood against the wall. And the spell that hit me on the way out? I understood its purpose now. I'd walked straight into it. Nicholas had used it to track me. He set his trap well.

"You lured me in," I whispered. "You knew I'd defend

you to the coven. You made me think they were the ones turning against you. It was the other way around, wasn't it? This whole time you've been working with The Ring?"

He shrugged. "It's where the real power is, Nadia. The coven system is archaic. We hand over decision making to the oldest, weakest members. The Ring lets power rest where it should. With the powerful."

I shook my head. "You know what they do. They traffic witches. They steal our power and twist it to their own ends. They've started wars between shifters and witches just to weaken them both."

"Pretty ingenious," the bald guy said. He came all the way down the stairs and stepped into the circle of light above my brother. He tilted his head, inspecting me.

"She's feisty," he said. "She'll fetch a pretty high price at auction. I've got a pair of buyers in mind already. If I could have a little taste, give them something to salivate over, I think I can start a bidding war."

Nicholas flinched. But then he nodded. He moved quickly. His eyes turned pitch black and he grabbed my wrist. Chaos swirled in my head. I felt like I was drowning. Then I felt another hand on my wrist. His grip was cold and clammy.

I found the strength to jerk away and fell back against the wall.

The bald guy had a wistful look and a sickening smile spread across his face.

"Oh, she'll do," he said. "We might set a record with this one."

My God. My brother was standing right in front of me. He looked like Nicholas. Sounded like him. But the brother I'd known back when we were kids was gone. Something evil had taken root inside of his soul. I'd been too trusting to see him for what he was all this time. And now it might be the end of me.

"Well, I've got a little secret," Nicholas said. "A bonus, if you will."

"Nicholas, don't," I said. "This isn't you."

"Oh it is," he said. "This is me finally fighting back and taking what is mine. Do you know what Michael told me? He said they were going to give you Dad's spot on the Council of Elders. After Uncle Cy refused it."

I shook my head. "What? You just said you don't believe in the council."

"So you would have been making decisions for me? I don't think so."

"Michael never told me that," I said. "Nicholas, you could have had it. I don't want the seat. You could have just told me."

"It doesn't matter," he said, his voice dripping with vitriol. "I don't want your sloppy seconds. You think anyone in the coven would have respected me if my sister handed me that seat? That would have been even worse than being passed over in the first place. So, I took what I wanted."

Nicholas was gone. Jealousy, raw dark power, maybe some new magic The Ring had used on him. I couldn't be sure. It was as if they'd hollowed out his soul and left this monster in its place.

"This is boring me," the bald man said. "You sure you can keep her under control during shipping?"

Shipping? I was a thing to them.

"Easy enough, Mr. Banning," he said. "The more she fights, the stronger the binding spell holds fast."

"How?" I said to Nicholas, ignoring Banning.

"You're predictable," he said. "I knew you'd believe whatever I told you. I knew you'd turn your back on the protection of the coven if you thought you were vindicating me. And you walked right into it. Stuck a locator spell on you. I knew you'd try to reconstruct the last moments of my so-called life."

"And I'd be vulnerable," I whispered. Nicholas had bided his time. When I was trying to control the dark magic from the Source, he brought me here. I never sensed it. The whole time I'd been looking to find someone else. His presence didn't trigger any alarm bells in me.

I'd been so stupid.

"Don't feel too bad," Nicholas said. "You put up a good fight. And as Mr. Banning here says, it'll be to your benefit. You're going to end up with a choice master. He'll probably treat you like a queen. If you behave."

"Master," I whispered.

So I was to be a witch slave for some member of The Ring. If I was lucky, all he'd do was force me to use my magic his way. I knew the stories about what happened to witch slaves. They never lived very long. Their masters would use their magic up until they went insane.

"You said you had a bonus," Banning said.

Nicholas smiled.

"Right," he said. "I saw something in the woods, right before I pulled her in. That shifter our coven sent to find her, he's something to her. She's his mate."

My heart dropped as Banning's eyes widened. He came to me. I jerked my chin back as he tried to run his fingers along my face.

"A shifter's mate?" he asked.

"A wolf shifter's mate," Nicholas answered. "One of the Kalenkovs."

Banning's eyes glistened. I thought I might be sick.

"We've had some run-ins with the Kalenkov wolves over the last year or so," Banning said. "This is interesting."

"I trust it'll up my finder's fee," Nicholas said.

Banning tilted his head and nodded. "It might."

"Come on," Nicholas said. "He's going to come after her."

"Hold her still," Banning said.

I tried to pull away. My brother's binding spell worked just as he said it would. The more I tried to use my magic to fight, the stronger it worked against me.

My skin crawled as Banning held my head. He pulled my hair away, looking for the mark at the base of my neck.

"That's a shame," he said. "He hasn't marked her yet."

"No," Nicholas said. "That's good luck. He'd have an easier time tracking her. Now you can leave your own trail of breadcrumbs and control this thing."

Banning let me go. "I see your point."

Nicholas sighed. "Do I have to tell you how to do everything? Put the word out. Tell your buyers you've got a Bach witch. You've sampled her power. And she's a

Kalenkov mate. We'll all be able to write our own tickets after that."

"I hate you," I whispered.

Nicholas put a hand over his heart, feigning a wound. "You'll get over it," he said.

Then, just like that, he snapped his fingers and pitched me into total darkness. I tried to run at him. My power snapped back, nearly choking me as I dropped to the floor.

CHAPTER SEVENTEEN

MILO

It took five of them to hold me down. I sank my fangs into Erik's shoulder. He delivered a sharp blow to my snout, making the stars spin.

Payne squatted down so his face was near mine. I panted, my claws digging into the ground and the flesh of the closest wolf.

"You want to do some good?" he said, barely able to keep from shifting himself. "Get a hold of it, man. You're useless in your wolf right now."

He whistled through two fingers. Three more men from Wolfguard broke through the trees. As my cousins Erik and Edward held me back with three other men, one of them a big-ass bear shifter with onion breath, I felt metal cuffs go around my ankles.

My spine cracked. The shift was instant, unstoppable.

They let me up then someone shoved me hard until my back was against a tree trunk.

"I'll kill you," I spat. Erik was the closest. His silver eyes glinted. His white-blond hair was pasted to his forehead with sweat.

"It's for your own good, man," he said. "You're not yourself. You need to listen to what we have to say for once."

I closed my eyes and reached out with my mind.

Nadia.

She was gone. I felt only my own thundering pulse. I saw her staring at me in my mind's eye just before she vanished, her expression filled with sadness.

She thought it was me. She thought I'd lied and called Wolfguard down on her.

I tried to shift. The manacles around my wrists and ankles held fast. Dragonsteel. The real stuff this time.

I arched my back and let out a howl that made everything in those woods with a pulse skitter in all directions. Except for the eight men who stood in front of me, their shifter eyes glowing with rage.

"Milo." Payne came forward. "You need to calm down."

"They'll kill her!" I shouted.

Payne narrowed his eyes. "Milo, they've been trying to protect her."

My nostrils flared. Even though I knew the Dragonsteel would keep me from shifting, I tried anyway. My muscles bunched and rolled. My head pounded.

"You're going to hurt yourself," Payne said.

"You're going to have to subjugate me," I spat. Snarling, I met Payne's eyes.

It was the gravest of insults. Only a *Tyrannous Alpha* would stoop to subjugating another wolf, let alone an Alpha without his consent. Payne had suffered under such a subjugation back in Kentucky. The scars he bore from it were buried.

He grabbed my face. "You know that's not who I am. You're not thinking clearly. We just saved your life!"

"What?"

"You weren't breathing," Erik said. "Milo, she hit you with something."

"A breathless spell." The voice came from deeper in the woods. He was an older man, maybe mid-fifties. His hair had gone pure white already. He had familiar, dark eyes and wore all black.

"A witch?" I said, bile rising in my throat. "You'd believe him over me?"

A breeze ruffled the man's black shirt. He stood next to Payne.

"My name is Cyrus," he said. "Cyrus Bach. I understand you've gotten to know my niece."

I looked from Payne to Erik. I believed the guy. Nadia shared some of his features. Those nearly black eyes, and straight, knife-bridge nose.

"Her coven isn't protecting her," I said. "They want her dead."

"You're right," Cyrus said. "But I'm no longer in the coven. I tried to do the right thing. Turns out I failed."

"She needs me," I said, still pulling against the Dragonsteel. God. I couldn't hear her. I couldn't feel her. I couldn't tell if it was the Dragonsteel shutting her away from me, or if she was gone for good.

Chaos swirled inside my head. If I lost her. If they hurt her ...

"Listen to me, son," Cyrus Bach said. "You were right about a lot of things. But Nadia's coven isn't the one who hired your firm. I am."

Payne had a hard set to his jaw. His silence confirmed Bach's statement.

"Why?" I asked.

"She's right that they turned on her. They turned on me too. I've used dark magic. But I'm not dark. They aren't the same thing."

"Her coven is in bed with The Ring," I said. "Every second we waste puts Nadia in more danger."

"No," Cyrus said. "I'm not going to defend the coven's actions. They've handled everything to do with Nicholas terribly. He could have been saved. If they'd sent him to me ..."

"You?" I said. "It was you. You killed your own nephew?"

Cyrus shook his head. "No, son."

"Stop calling me that."

He shrugged. "The coven isn't in bed with The Ring. Only Nicholas was. I should have seen it in him a long time ago. You know, my brother warned me. Before he died he told me to watch out for Nicholas. He was volatile even as a young boy. My brother thought he was too much like me."

Cyrus March smiled. His face took on a wistful expression.

"I don't have time for your bullshit stories," I said. "You either need to kill me or let me go. I am going after Nadia."

"Of course you are," Cyrus said. "And that's exactly what they expect."

"Milo," Payne said. "I'm sorry I couldn't be completely forthright with you about who hired us. I was sworn to secrecy. And in this case, I believe it was warranted."

"Nadia has been trying to figure out who killed her brother," I said. "That's all she's ever wanted."

A look passed between Cyrus and Payne. I pulled against the bindings even harder.

"Milo," Edward stepped forward. He leaned down to me. "Just listen to what they have to say. I know this is hard."

"You don't know anything," I said. "And after this, you're dead to me. You and Erik both. And any man who tried to stand in the way of me getting to Nadia. You used me. You have no idea what she is to me. But you ... Payne ... you do. Your wife, Lena, she's your fated mate. You've done what I have and more to protect her. You know what this is."

Payne nodded. "I do. But you don't understand what's at play here. Nadia is the one who's been using you. She may not have even realized she was doing it. Her connection to her brother was stronger than we realized."

"Than I realized," Cyrus said. "That's where I made my mistake. Nicholas has been a step ahead of me. That's on me."

"Nicholas?" I said.

There was that look again between Payne and Cyrus.

"No one killed Nicholas," Cyrus said. "It was all an illusion. He staged it to lure Nadia away from the protection of her coven."

My mind reeled. "You knew this? You *knew* it? And you let her go after him?"

Cyrus shook his head. "I didn't know until tonight. Not until she cast that spell. I suspected The Ring would try to make contact with either Nicholas or Nadia. They've been trying to procure a Bach for generations. I thought by leaving the coven, I'd draw them away from those two. I was wrong."

"Procure a Bach," I repeated.

I knew what it meant, but I couldn't form the words. We'd known for some time now that members of The Ring had been "collecting" shifters' mates and betas. It made sense they'd go after witches too.

"Our line is the strongest of the wind mages," Cyrus said. "I'm so sorry. I really was trying to protect her by hiring you all to find her."

"*I* was protecting her," I said through gritted teeth.

"She's too far gone," Cyrus said. "What she did to Michael ..."

"It's a lie!" I said. "That footage you have. It was another trick. If Nicholas is alive, then he's probably the one who cast it. Michael tried to hurt Nadia. She said what you saw on that tape isn't how it happened. Michael was at the window. He cast a spell and she defended herself."

Cyrus scratched his chin. "It's possible. Nicholas could

have been nearby. He might have known Nadia would go to Michael if he summoned her. It's a simple spell really. Kind of ingenious ..."

"Enough," I said. "You're telling me Nadia's brother has been behind all of this? He's capable of selling his own sister to The Ring?"

Cyrus nodded. "Yes. That's what I'm telling you. I should have seen it. Nicholas was always jealous of Nadia. He was jealous of everyone. He kept her close to him. Made her mistrust me, Michael, anyone else who tried to get close to her. I have my suspicions now that we know what that boy is capable of. I think it's possible he's behind their parents' deaths as well. Sofia died in a car accident when the kids were little. My brother got sick. Cancer. But maybe it was magic-based. I never thought to check. Anyway, Nicholas would have been next in line to take a leadership position in the coven when I left. But I recommended against it. I knew his temperament was an issue. There are so many things I could have done differently."

"You can undo it now," I said. "Let me go. If Nadia's still out there, I'm the only one with a shot at finding her."

"It's a suicide mission," Erik said. "Don't you get it?"

"They'll be expecting that," Cyrus said. "You didn't mark her, did you?"

I dropped my head. "No. That's the thing I should have done differently."

"Hmm," Cyrus said. "Nicholas is smart enough to figure out she's your fated mate though. He'll use it to up the bid price for her."

I growled and drove a fist into the bark of the tree,

splintering it.

"They know you'll come after her," Payne said. "It's an easy trap to set."

"I don't care," I said. "I'll die with her if that's the only thing left."

"No!" Erik and Edward shouted in unison. I was far past appreciating their familial concern. I needed it days ago.

"How do we get to her?" Payne asked Cyrus.

"You don't," Cyrus said. "This is The Ring we're talking about."

"My men have gone up against them before," Payne said. "And won."

"You don't understand how important it is to them having a wind mage of Nadia's power under their control. We're not talking about some human woman some shifter wants for a slave. Or trinkets or whatever other run-ins you've had with them."

Payne's wolf simmered just below his skin. How the hell did Cyrus Bach know so much about our dealings with The Ring?

"I'm sorry," Payne said to me. "I know what I'm doing to you. And I know you'll never be able to forgive me for it. But I won't let you go after her like this. We need a better plan. We need time."

I roared. Blood poured from my wrists as I strained against the metal cuffs.

Cyrus lifted an amused brow. "Unfortunately," he said. "Time's the one thing we don't have."

He raised his arms. His eyes glinted with blue fire. In

the time it took him to draw a breath, the sky opened up. A tornado touched down, tearing the tops off the trees. Only Cyrus and I remained in the eye of it. Payne, my cousins, and all the other men from Wolfguard were flung wildly backward.

Cyrus knelt down to me.

"I'm going to let you go," he said. "You know your friends are right. You probably won't survive this."

"I don't care," I said. "You know I have to go to her."

He nodded. "I'm counting on it. I'll help you if I can. But it won't be much."

"You know where they've taken her?" I asked.

"I think so. I know a bit of magic that can help with that. If you're really bonded to her, your magic will do the rest. Might make you dizzy for a second. It should wear off."

"Should?" I shouted.

Cyrus shrugged.

"Never mind. Get on with it. What about them?" I asked. The shifters had all been thrown hundreds of yards away. Cyrus's spell knocked them out, but it wouldn't last.

"Oh, they'll be out for a minute or so. Might wake up with a bit of a headache, but none the worse for wear."

I lifted my wrists. Cyrus cocked his head to the side. He drew another breath and the manacles around my wrists and ankles unlocked.

I rose, towering over Cyrus Bach. He drew one more breath and a blast of air hit me in the chest. The ground seemed to open up and swallow me. I fell backward and down into nothingness.

CHAPTER EIGHTEEN

NADIA

"I never knew you hated me so much," I said. Nicholas sat beside me in the back of the sedan they'd thrown me into. My hands were bound with glowing blue cuffs. He'd also blindfolded me and whatever spell he'd used on the cloth made me dizzy.

"Nadia," he said, exasperated. "I don't hate you. You've always been so shortsighted. I'm doing this for us."

"Us," I said. "How is selling me to some power broker in The Ring good for us, Nicholas?"

"Covens are dying, little sister. It's an archaic system. Weren't you listening? When the new world comes, people like Michael Tolliver, Uncle Cy, they'll be left to rot in the dust. But us? We'll be connected at the top levels. You'll see."

"We," I said. "You mean you. Nicholas, we both know

what these men do to women like me. You keep me bound like this and I won't be able to defend myself."

"Don't be so dramatic," he said. "You'll live like a queen. Your new benefactor will make sure you'll want for nothing. And for doing essentially nothing in return. You give him a taste of your juice every once in a while. Just one little connection to The Source to feed his habit. Sometimes maybe his friends. But these guys aren't stupid. They hurt you, they hurt their supply. That's bad for business."

"You know what happens to witches who get used like that," I said. "Just to provide a cheap high to some spell-head. You lose something when it's taken like that. It's not natural. You'd let them hollow me out. Let me be tortured and trapped for what, weeks?"

"You're strong, Nadia. God knows I've had to listen to that my whole life. Someone like you, a Bach ... the strongest Bach. You'll last a decade, easy."

My tears wet the blindfold. I felt like I was going to be sick. My pulse thundered in my ears but it felt so raw and empty. I couldn't sense Milo anymore.

Milo. He looked shocked when the men from Wolf-guard surrounded me. How could I have trusted him? Was he just one more man who'd sold me out?

Except deep in my soul, I didn't want to believe it. He was real. You couldn't fake what we were to each other. I had to believe he didn't know what was going to happen, even if it was naive. But I'd had my trust used against me time and again. Now my own brother had reached out and used my magic to hurt me. I hadn't realized he'd grown so powerful. He'd never been able to complete a translocation spell before.

The car came to a stop. My heart hurt from beating so hard. The door opened beside me and I was jerked from the seat.

"Wait here," a gruff voice said.

I tried not to panic. If I could stay calm, I might find a chance. Maybe one brief moment where I could tap into The Source and use wind. They couldn't keep me bound like this forever. Whoever Nicholas planned to sell me to would need me to be able to access my magic if he planned to steal some of it. Then I could show them just how powerful my Bach blood really ran.

"Are we alone?" I asked.

"For now," Nicholas said. For the first time, I sensed uncertainty in his voice.

"What makes you think they'll give a rat's ass what happens to you once this transaction is complete?" I asked. "I'm the only sister you have."

His fingers were rough as he grabbed my arms. "You might be one of the best finds I bring them, but you won't be the last. The Ring rewards loyalty. And you'd be wise to show me respect and a little gratitude."

"Go to hell," I said. "I loved you. What do you think Mom and Dad would do to you if they were still here?"

He snorted. "They're both where they belong. In the ground where I put them."

His words hit me like a fresh blow to the heart. He killed them too. My God. My brother had forced me to wear a blindfold of a different kind for half my life.

"Change is coming," Nicolas said. "Everything's already in motion. The covens, wolf packs, bear clans, they won't exist anymore, Nadia. You just don't get it. The Ring is the way. And thanks to me, you'll have a place in it. Everything I've done I've done because I *do* love you. And it matters to me that you survive in the new world This way, because of what we do here today, you will."

I heard footsteps. I stepped backward, moving behind my brother on instinct. He grabbed me again and shoved me forward. I nearly stumbled.

We walked for a while. The concrete beneath my feet turned to grass. I smelled the woods again, pungent and fresh. I felt the wind on my face and tried to bring it into me. The bindings on my wrists kept me from it. They were imbued with strong, dark magic. I suspected Nicholas was borrowing magic to amplify his own.

Then Nicholas let me go.

"This is her?" a gravelly voice asked. He was tall, standing right in front of me. I nearly choked on the scent of thick cologne.

"She's pure," Nicholas said. "Never been tapped."

I wanted to be sick.

"I'll need proof," the man said.

"The bindings on her wrist are spellbound," Nicholas said. "If I let her go, she'll try to fight. She'll probably kill you. But I can open a port. Until you train her, you're going to need me around to do this whenever you want a taste."

"You son of a bitch," I spat at my brother. So this was how he planned to save his own neck for the time being. He would help these men rape my power until they'd taken so much it would be harder for me to fight back.

It happened so fast. Nicholas kept a hand on my arm. The other man curled his fingers around my other arm. The power flowed through me. It was violent, dizzying. Maddening.

Then it was over. I staggered to the side and threw up.

"Nice," the man said. "Real nice."

He sounded drunk.

"It gets even better," Nicholas said.

I heard more footsteps. "We've named our price." It was Banning. "Now we're going to double it."

"The hell you will," the man said.

"Circumstances have changed," Banning said. "The girl has some more specials we didn't anticipate. She's a wolf shifter's mate."

Rough fingers grabbed my hair. The man bent me forward so he could look at my neck.

"I see no mark," he said.

"She belongs to Milo Kalenkov. I trust you recognize the name?"

Low, sick laughter.

"He hasn't gotten around to marking her," Nicholas said. "But you can be sure he will try. If you play your cards right, there's bigger game you can catch. You control her, you control Milo Kalenkov. You know who his father is, I take it?"

"Nicholas!" I shouted.

Banning and the man moved off. They spoke in hushed whispers; I couldn't make out the words.

"You're going to pay," I said to my brother.

"I'm going to *be* paid," he said. "Handsomely. And quit acting like I'm turning you out like some whore. This is a privilege, what you're getting."

"All right." The man came back. "I'll agree to your new price. But I'm going to need proof this girl is who you say she is. And I don't want it landing on me. You put the word out. Set the trap. And *you* capture the wolf. I don't need the aggravation."

"We don't offer free shipping, Seamus," Banning said dryly.

"I need proof she's his," the man Seamus said. "If she's really his, Kalenkov won't stop until he finds her. When that happens ..."

There was a rush of air. I smelled blood. A scream.

Strong hands pushed me sideways. I fell to the ground hard, landing on my hip.

I brought my hands up. I couldn't access my magic, but I could pull at my blindfold.

Seamus screamed. My brother stood beside him, his hands up, the wind lifting his hair. Squaring off in front of them was one keyed-up black wolf, fangs dripping.

Milo.

"Don't be stupid," Nicholas said.

Seamus threw a punch. He was still high from the bit of magic he stole from me. Milo's wolf dodged it.

Nicholas threw a spell, landing a phantom blow against Milo's head. He staggered to the right, yelping. But he recovered and charged Nicholas.

I got to my feet. We were in a field. The cars were

parked on a hill above us. I scrambled up to the road, looking for something I could use to pry open the bindings on my wrist.

There was nothing there but a metal guardrail. I raised my wrists and brought them down hard. The cuffs were made of standard steel. They could be broken. With my brother busy trying to protect Seamus, he might have trouble keeping his spell in place.

I succeeded in putting a dent in the cuffs. I brought the chain down hard on the guardrail again and again.

Banning joined the melee. He wasn't a shifter, but I sensed more borrowed magic in him. I prayed for the witch he'd stolen it from.

Nicholas threw another bolt of magic across Milo's back. It opened up an ugly gash in his fur. Blood poured forth but didn't slow him down.

I got my wrists under the guardrail, finding its sharpest edge. I scraped the chain against it.

I saw my brother take a few steps back. He raised his arms and drew in a great breath. I knew what he was trying to do. He meant to throw a breathless spell straight at Milo.

"Milo, now!" I screamed. "Hit him now!"

As my brother drew in air, he was at his most vulnerable. If Milo could knock him out, even for a split second, it would be enough for me to break the magic on the chains. I ran toward them.

Milo rounded. He flew through the air. He landed hard against my brother's chest, knocking him backward with bone-crunching strength.

I drew in air of my own.

The chains fell to the ground as if they were made of paper. The air was mine.

I levitated ten feet off the ground. The world turned blue and gold. I saw the men beneath me. My brother writhed on the ground.

Milo's wolf darted out of the circle, taking a position behind me.

Then I became the storm.

A blast of heat and air moved through me. It knocked into Nicholas, Banning, and Seamus, throwing them back, ripping the grass from the earth. My wind made a crater in the ground.

I landed hard on all fours. Milo was at my side. He shifted and scrambled to me.

"Nadia," he gasped. I was in his arms.

"You came," I cried. "Milo, they were going to kill you."

It was true. He would have hurt them. Maybe killed them. But Banning had a weapon. It lay on the ground beside us, its blade twisted now.

Milo picked it up. It was Dragonsteel. A dagger. One jab and he could have killed Milo in an instant.

Seamus was the first to try and move. His back was broken and bent. Milo shifted again. He sank his fangs into Seamus's neck. The man would never get up again.

"Nicholas," I said.

Milo howled. A moment passed. Then three SUVs pulled up behind the cars on the hill.

"Friends," Milo said. "Wolfguard."

He came to me. Milo's arms were strong and solid around me as the men from Wolfguard sprang into action.

They'd brought Dragonsteel of their own.

Banning was on the ground, not moving. Only Nicholas seemed to have vanished into thin air.

"Are you okay?" Milo asked. He'd pulled a pair of jeans out of the trunk of one of the Wolfguard vehicles. I leaned against the side of it.

"You came," I said again. "Milo, I meant what I said. They would have killed you."

He hooked a finger beneath my chin and raised my gaze to his. "Then I would have died for you. There was never any choice."

He came. They'd told him I was dark. They'd shown him the evidence. He'd gone against his family. Against Wolfguard. All for me.

Because there was never any choice.

"Come on, my love," he said as he kissed me. "I want to introduce you to the family."

CHAPTER NINETEEN

MILO

She held my heart. I held her hand. Erik and Edward had embraced her, welcoming her into the Kalenkov family without so much as a word from me. Though I hated to let her go for even a second, there was still business to finish.

"I'm fine," Nadia said. She sat in the back seat of Payne's SUV, a blanket wrapped around her shoulders. Her wind spell had taken something out of her, but she was quickly regaining her strength. God, she was so stunning. So fierce. I knew in my soul I'd have the rest of my life to uncover all of her secrets.

Payne and the others waited for me in the van. An extraction team had taken Banning into custody. The man Nadia knew as Seamus died where I left him. The team had just finished zipping him into a body bag.

I closed the van door behind me. Payne was on a headset. He clicked off and faced me.

"Any sign of Cyrus Bach?" I asked. After he'd zapped me here, I lost all track of him. Nadia said the translocation spell would have taken a lot out of him. She guessed he was holed up somewhere, resting. I shuddered to think what would have happened if he hadn't been able to pull it off. If I hadn't made it to Nadia in time ...

"None," Payne said. "I have a hunch the old guy will turn up when he wants to be found."

"Or never," Erik said.

"We owe him," I said.

"And we won't forget it," Payne said. "You okay?"

"As long as Nadia is."

Payne nodded. With a fated mate himself, he knew what I felt.

"I should have listened to you sooner," he said. "I'll be forever sorry for that.'

"It doesn't matter now," I said. "She's the only thing that does. But I need your assurances that Nadia has Wolf-guard's full protection. Seamus may be dead, but The Ring might try again. For all we know, Nicholas Bach is still out there somewhere plotting another way to get to his sister."

My wolf stirred. I would kill him when I got the chance.

"I swear to you," Payne said. "Wolfguard will prioritize finding him. The Ring knows what will happen if they try for her again. I suspect they're going to decide she's not worth the risk."

"I hope so," I said.

"You did good," Payne said. "This is how we're going to defeat The Ring over time. One case at a time. With any luck, Banning will talk when he recovers. I've got alliances of my own with a few coven elders. As soon as they're made aware of what happened here today, all hell's going to break loose. I'd say Nadia is the most high profile target The Ring could try to procure. They can't chance bringing Wolf-guard and every coven in North America down on their heads."

"Or the Kalenkov pack," Erik said. "Nadia is one of ours now too."

I swallowed hard. Erik locked eyes with me. The bond between us was strong and unbreakable. He'd just pledged his life for Nadia's if it came to it. It meant everything.

"You've earned some time off," Payne said.

"I want to be part of Banning's debriefing," I said.

Payne nodded. "Of course. It's going to take some time. You owe yourself, and Nadia, a few days of peace and solitude. I suggest you take it."

Yes. Payne understood me on a different level now. I was grateful.

"Go," he said. "The Waterfall Glen area is secure. I had a hunch that's where you'd want to take her."

There was a knowing glint in Payne's eyes. I extended my hand and shook his. My wolf was itching to move. He gave me the keys to his SUV.

"I've arranged for a detail," he said. "They'll be close by if you need them, but far enough away you won't see or hear them. All throughout Waterfall Glen. The cabin is unoccupied."

"Thank you," I said. "And you'll call me about Banning."

Payne nodded. It was time for me to go. I said goodbye to my cousins. We'd have new work to do soon enough. For now, Nadia was all that mattered.

By the time I got back to her, she was curled up asleep in the back of the car. I gently closed the door and slipped behind the wheel. There was a six-hour drive between here and the Waterfall Glen area of Illinois. Nadia slept the whole way.

The nature preserve in the heart of Illinois was home to me. I owned land just outside of Darien. It was more home to me now than any place in Russia. But this place reminded me a little of Siberia in the winter. I hoped to be able to come back here later in the year to show that side of it to Nadia.

For now, I parked the car alongside the log cabin hideaway Wolfguard owned. I rented this space to them. A few miles to the east, I owned my own plot of land along a hidden lake. I'd always dreamed of building a house there, but never found the right time.

Turns out it wasn't time I was waiting for. It was Nadia.

"Where are we?" she asked, yawning.

"Home," I said. "If you want it to be."

Nadia came to stand beside me. It was nearly dusk. She gasped as she looked out at the lush green forest beyond the rolling hills.

"I know this place," she said. "I think I've seen it in a dream. I was standing near the water's edge. And you were there. I saw your wolf in silhouette, your face was reflected in the water."

I smiled and pulled her against me. "That sounds perfect. And I think I know the place. Are you up for it? We can go into the cabin. We have electricity and running water. You can ..."

"Later," she said, smiling up at me. "I'm hungry for something else now."

I let out a growl. Nadia dropped the blanket she'd held around her shoulders. A slight breeze lifted her hair.

That night, I felt like I could fly. She followed me. We took the trail through the woods. It was a long way, but Nadia never tired. I found the spot where I'd build the house. It was covered in dense trees now. Tonight, that was perfect for us.

Nadia spread the blanket on the ground. Smiling, she unbuttoned her jeans and slid them off. I stepped back and watched her, growing rigid.

Her hair lifted around her shoulders. It was her wind tonight, joined with the gentle rhythm of the trees. She belonged here. Her skin flushed. Nipples like dark cherries, waiting to be sucked.

Nadia held her arms out, beckoning me.

I went to her, sliding my hands over her back, then downward until I cupped her round ass.

"Kiss me," she whispered.

She tasted so good. Sweet. I could get drunk from her. Nadia unzipped my jeans. I kicked them off. Her hands were on me, gentle fingers curving around my erection.

Then Nadia went to her knees. She took me in her mouth. The air was cool, but she was hot and wet, drawing me out with delicious swirls of her tongue. Soft, then hard. She found the perfect suction.

I threaded my hands through her hair, spurring her on. I spread my legs, planting my feet wide as she kept up her pace.

She tasted me, then took me in. All of me. Never missing a drop.

Then it was my turn. Nadia went to all fours. I gave her a playful swat on the ass that made her squeal with delight. I gently spread her folds and tasted her.

I loved the little gasps she made as I drew her out. I teased her just enough, watching her squirm. Then I plunged inside of her, becoming merciless with lips and tongue.

She came for me. Her cries of ecstasy echoed through the woods. We were only just beginning.

Nadia rolled to her back. I took her by the ankles; lifting upward I spread her impossibly wide.

"Yes," she gasped.

I made her mine, sheathing myself to the root. I found a punishing rhythm. Nadia clawed at my back, pulling me into her ever deeper.

I claimed her.

"Mine," I growled. "Say it."

"Yes," she said, her voice hitching.

"Say it! I want the whole world to hear you."

"Milo," she cried out; she was already in the throes of another, even more powerful orgasm.

"Say it or I'll stop," I teased. Then I did. I held myself still buried inside of her.

Nadia's eyes snapped open. "Please!" she shouted, clawing at me again. She tried to thrust her hips but I held her in place.

"Say it, if you want more," I whispered. I nipped her calf as I held her leg over my shoulder.

"Yes," she whimpered. "Milo, yes. I'm yours."

"Louder."

"I'm yours!" she panted. "All yours. Always. All of me."

"This?" I asked, pressing a finger to her lips.

"Yes," she whispered. I kissed her.

"This?" I asked, cupping her ass.

"Oh yes!" she said.

"This?" I asked, swirling my tongue around each of her nipples. She arched her back in response.

"Yes!"

I reached between her legs and gently tapped her hard little bud. She was stretched wide where I entered her.

"This?" I asked, letting my fangs drop a little. I snapped my jaw.

"Mmm." She was barely verbal.

I let out a wicked laugh. "Not good enough, my love." I gave her sex a gentle squeeze. She gushed all over me.

"This?"

"Yes!" She found her voice, bucking wild beneath me. "Yes! It's yours!"

She came for me, her orgasm ripping out of her. I held on for the ride.

As she crested down, I kissed the space just above her breasts where her heart beat strongest in time with my own.

"This?" I whispered.

"Yes," she said, eyes sparking. "Forever."

Then I slid out of her. I helped Nadia to her knees and guided her down until she rested her chin on her hands. I stroked her from behind, drawing more of her juices out.

"Please," she said. "I want it. Milo, I need it."

So did I.

I slipped inside of her easily now. I braced one hand on her hip then leaned far forward. Nadia's hair fell to the side.

I licked a trail between her shoulder blades, coming to a stop at the base of her neck. My fangs were fully out now.

"This?" I said.

She wept with pleasure. "Yes. Oh God. Yes."

The wind kicked up. Once again, we were in the eye of the storm. Nadia's magic joined with mine, bending the trees at their very tips. Leaves kicked up around us but never touched us. Nadia was in control of her power as I was of mine.

I took a breath, then plunged my fangs into that space at the base of her neck. She felt it as a split second of pain, then blossoming pleasure.

I came inside of her at the same instant as I made my mark. We were one. The circle was complete.

Nadia came violently, shuddering around me as she was reborn. My true mate. The mark I made began to heal before the last spasm of her climax. I pulled her against me, cradling her with my body.

"Oh, Milo," she whispered. "It was better than my dreams."

I smiled. "It always is. And that's just the start."

She turned, facing me. I couldn't keep my hands off her. We kissed. I cupped her breasts. I marveled at every inch of her.

Mine. All mine. And she owned me just as much.

The breeze settled, becoming quiet and still. It was as if the world fell away and there was only just the two of us.

"I love you," I said. "No matter what happens next, I'll make you safe."

She touched my cheek. "I'm not afraid of anything, Milo. I love you so much it hurts."

I kissed her palm. "Good," I said. "Then marry me."

Her face lit with a smile. "My God!"

"Marry me," I said again.

She answered with a kiss and her growing need. Oh yes. I would take her again and again this night and every day after.

Her power made mine stronger. Her heart was my heart. We said our vows under the light of the moon.

CHAPTER TWENTY

Milo

One week later ...

I paced outside the examination room. If it weren't for Nadia's stern words in my head, I might have busted through the damn door.

I'm fine. He can't hurt me. We're doing good work here. I'll be out in a minute.

I loved having her in my mind as much as my bed. In the days since I first marked her, I'd done it again. Our bond grew at a rapid pace. It was all because of Nadia. Her magic amplified the connection. I knew what that meant and she'd accepted it so willingly.

Sooner rather than later, my Nadia would be in full heat. We'd bring a shifter into the world with the power of the wind. Our child would be magnificent.

But today, I was forced to wait outside while four of the

most powerful mages in the world tried to bend
Bartholomew Banning's mind to their will.

For my part, I just wanted to kill him.

The door opened. Nadia looked pale. I went to her, my
wolf rushing to the surface. A simple touch from her
calmed me.

Nadia said a few words to the other mages. One was an
earth mage from a Canadian coven. She was at least
seventy but walked with sure purpose and stood over six
feet tall.

Nadia had called in a fire mage from California,
Gemma Brandhart. My sister Grace vouched for her.
Gemma was married to another of the Brandhart dragons.
That made her Grace's sister-in-law.

The last was a water mage sent from Martinique. She
only spoke French but words weren't required for what
these four tried.

Payne and Erik came down the hall. Nadia said her
goodbyes to the others then we followed Payne into one of
the empty conference rooms. This was the Chicago head-
quarters of Wolfguard. My home base.

Payne took a seat. I held Nadia's hand as we sat opposite him. Erik stayed on his feet. He was agitated, ready to
take off on a new assignment. There was trouble among a
group of jaguar shifters down in Texas.

"He's wiped clean," Nadia said.

The lines in Payne's face deepened. "What do you
mean wiped?"

"Well," she said. "My theory is Nicholas did it. I felt
something go through me right before he vanished. He cast

a spell aimed for Banning. Wiped his memory. We tried everything we could. He's not under the influence of an active spell now. Whatever my brother did was meant to injure him permanently."

"Dammit," Payne said. "I was afraid of that."

"He's lucky he didn't erase some of his basic functions. Banning can still talk. He's otherwise neurologically intact. He just can't remember who he is or anything about his life before he woke up in that field."

"You're sure it won't wear off in time?"

Nadia shrugged. "Personally, no. I don't. But maybe someday, if we ever find Nicholas ..."

"Then you'd have to force him to help you," I said.

"Right," she said. "That'll never happen. Nicholas kept talking about securing his place with The Ring for when the new order or world ... something ... happens. I think he hoped to score points by rendering Banning useless to us even though he was captured. My brother took a live-to-fight-another-day approach."

"You're sure he's alive then?" I asked.

"No," she said. "Nicholas fooled me before. I'm not sure of anything where he's concerned."

"You've been restored to your coven," Payne asked.

She nodded. "Yes. I've taken a place on the council. But I'll be living away from them for now. Maybe forever."

She smiled and squeezed my hand. Payne's face lightened. Even Erik cracked a smile.

"Did you tell Uncle Andre yet?" Erik asked.

"Nadia and I are going to take some time off. We'll fly to Moscow next week so I can talk to my father face to face.

After that, I'm starting construction on the house in Darien."

"Congratulations," Payne said. "You let me know if there's anything I can do to help."

"There is," I said. My eyes met Nadia's. I wasn't sure how Payne would take my next request.

"I'd like to make some changes," I said. "I'm not sure fieldwork is what I'm interested in ..."

Payne put a hand up. "Milo," he said. "Before you go on. Don't. That's the other thing I wanted to talk to you about today. I need you. But in a different way. I know we've got some dark days ahead of us as The Ring tries to push back. So, I need you here. In this office. Milo, I want you to run it. It's a desk job. But you'll be coordinating all the units based in Chicago. Nadia, if you're up for it, I could use you here too. We need a magic consultant."

Nadia's smile widened. It was more than we ever could have hoped for. Payne was giving me my own branch.

"I'd like that," she said. "The commute from Darien is only what, thirty minutes? Or I mean ... I could just zap us."

Payne looked horrified but I knew she was teasing. I brought Nadia's hand to my lips and kissed it.

"We accept," I said.

"I've said this to Milo," Payne said. "But Nadia, I hope you know you've got the full protection of Wolfguard at your disposal. Your brother is still a question mark. I'm sorry about that. We'll help in any way we can. You'll never be vulnerable to The Ring again. Although, you've proven you're more than capable of taking care of yourself."

"Thank you," she said. "Oddly, I'm not worried about Nicholas anymore. He's nowhere near as powerful as I am and he knows it. Plus, despite what he did to Banning, I think he's got bigger problems from The Ring than I do. They wanted to procure a Bach mage. Well, Nicholas is a Bach mage, even if he isn't me. It seems to me their easiest path forward is using him for whatever they wanted from me. Part of me feels sorry for him. But I did all I could for him. He's chosen his fate. And I've chosen mine."

Nadia leaned in and kissed me. My heart swelled.

"Gross," Erik said, teasing. "Would you two just go on and ... do whatever mates do ... the rest of us need to work for a living."

I rose and faked a punch at my cousin. Then I pulled him into a hug.

"Be careful out there," I said. "And don't be afraid to call for Kalenkov backup when you need it. I owe you, cousin."

"I think I owe you more," he said, winking at Nadia.

Then the meeting was over. Payne congratulated us again. He handed me a key card to the penthouse offices. My jaw dropped as he slapped me on the back.

After they left, Nadia and I rode the elevator all the way up to the twenty-seventh floor. From there, we had a panoramic view of the city. There was a suite of offices, but also a spacious apartment. I took her there.

Nadia and I looked out at the stunning vista of Chicago's Gold Coast. She leaned against me and I kissed her neck.

"You know," I said. "If you prefer city life ..."

"No," she said. "It has its charms, but we belong in the woods, my love."

I let out a sigh of relief. It's what I wanted too. There was another need growing strong as I held her against me.

"Milo!" she gasped. "We just did that this morning!"

She was teasing. Even now I could feel her rising heat. I slid my fingers beneath the bodice of her dress and found her nipples already pebbled hard for me. She turned in my arms and kissed me.

"Come on," I said. "Let's christen the new office."

Then we did.

CHAPTER TWENTY-ONE

FIVE MONTHS LATER ...
NADIA

"My brother is going to lose his mind," Milo's sister, Grace, said.

She fastened the clasp in the back of my dress. It was pure silk with delicate lace at the waist. My mother wore it on her wedding day to my father twenty-five years ago. I missed her today, though my memories of her had started to fade. Still, I felt her with me.

Grace had tears in her eyes. I'd never had a sister before. Meeting her had been the biggest blessing in my life after finding Milo.

We almost looked like sisters, in fact. Our dark hair matched. But Grace was far taller than I. Though she was human, she had shifter blood in her.

"You look like a queen," she whispered. She handed me

my bouquet of lilies. Grace herself looked stunning in a yellow strapless gown. Her daughter Amelia was just old enough to serve as my flower girl. Milo's father, Andre Kalenkov, the mighty Siberian Alpha himself, would walk me down the aisle. He cut a dashing figure as he came to the doorway.

"Are you ready, daughters?" he said in his clipped Russian accent. He was smiling.

My heart fluttered. I felt Milo's pulse quicken with it.

"You look beautiful," Andre said. "Your father is looking down on you today. You know this?"

"I do," I said. "Now stop it, you're going to make me cry."

His own nose reddened. Grace went on her tiptoes to kiss her father.

"Let's go," he said, offering me his strong arm.

Andre had the same inner heat all wolf shifters had. Sometimes it was like standing next to a blast furnace. But today, the warmth comforted me. I felt my own growing heat in my core.

As soon as Andre's fingers touched my arm, his eyes widened. He sensed something too and tears made his eyes glisten.

"Already?" he asked.

I put a finger to my lips. "Shh. I'll tell everyone after."

Grace looked back. She had a knowing smile.

"I hate to break it to you, sister," she said. "But you're walking down a gauntlet of wolf shifters and their mates. We all know what that glow in your cheeks means. How far along?"

I swallowed past a lump in my throat and put a hand over my still-flat belly.

"About three months," I said. "We were going to tell everybody at the party."

"Perfect," Grace said.

I still had one secret. It was Milo who felt it first. He said it came to him in a dream. When he spoke it aloud I knew it was true.

A son. After the first of the year, I would give birth to Milo Kalenkov's son. His wolf would be silver just like his father's. I could see his golden eyes too. But I saw something else I hadn't yet told Milo. Our boy was also a Bach. He would be strong with wind magic. And he would do something extraordinary. I couldn't wait to find out what.

"Come on," Andre said. "We go!"

So we did. Milo had arranged for a string quartet to play as his father walked me down the aisle.

Amelia spread yellow rose petals in front of us. My breath caught as another vision struck me. I saw Amelia playing with her cousin, my son. She would help him grow into his power, be his guide, as close to him as a sister. Amelia was special. Her birth had broken a curse. She was a full-blooded wolf shifter. She would grow to be fierce and powerful, and she and her cousin would be a dominant force in the world.

And someday, my son would leave us and I knew at once what I would call him.

We would name him after his grandfather. Though it tugged at my heart a bit to think of him so far away, I knew with complete clarity that one day, young Andre would take his grandfather's place and lead the largest wolf shifter pack in the world.

But those were all stories for another day. Today, I would write my happy beginning.

One guest stood off to the side, away from the rest of the crowd. My Uncle Cyrus gave me a knowing smile. He looked handsome and so like my father in his tux. I was grateful to him, but still mistrustful. Instinct told me Uncle Cy still held secrets of his own. But he was here today. He showed up. Later, he'd give me a hug then disappear, skipping the party. I had a hunch I wouldn't see him again for a very long time, if ever.

Then my attention left my uncle's gaze. Milo stood at the end of the white carpet. We chose the spot where he first marked me, though that was our secret.

The summer sun hung high in a pure azure sky as I let go of Andre and stepped into Milo's arms.

My wolf. My handsome, strong, noble wolf.

The minister said words. I felt them, even if I don't remember all of them. I pledged myself to Milo in front of my coven. My uncle. His father's pack. The men and women of Wolfguard, and the hidden lake where we'd built our home.

"I love you, Mrs. Kalenkov," he said to me later. It sounded so good.

"Not as much as I love you," I said.

"Are you sad at all?" he asked.

"Sad?" I drew away from him. We sat on a bench overlooking the lake. The party went on into the early morning. The last guests were just starting to leave.

"You've lost so much," he said. I sensed his next words.

"Don't," I said. Today, I didn't want to hear my brother's name. He was gone. Truly gone. Maybe not dead, but I knew he'd been cut off from The Source. My coven and I had seen to it. Nicholas could still try to tap into dark magic, but I knew he wasn't strong enough to survive it for long. He couldn't hurt me again.

"I've gained everything I'll ever need, my love," I said. He put a hand over my stomach. Then he leaned down and kissed me there.

"They all know," I said, giggling.

Milo raised a brow. "Are you serious?"

"Yep. I didn't tell them we know it's a boy though. You can save that secret for later."

"Hmm," he said. "You're happy?"

"Milo, I'm more than happy. I'm home."

And I was. Home was something I never knew I missed. I never realized I never had. But now, I knew where I belonged.

"Come here, witch," he said.

"Kiss me, wolf," I answered.

He did. In the distance, the rest of the Kalenkov wolves raised a chorus of howls. Their nature called to them and they shifted; tearing through the trees they went to the hill overlooking the lake.

I felt Milo's wolf stir, aching to join them. Then, deep in my core, I felt the first fluttering movement of my new son. He felt the call of the wolves too, it seemed.

"Go," I whispered. "Wolf out. I'll wait right here for you."

"Wolf out?" he said. I flapped a dismissive hand. I'd kicked off my shoes and dangled my toes in the water. "Just don't be long."

"I promised I won't leave you alone for long. When I get back, we can seal our vows in a deeper way." Desire flooded me as he nipped my ear. He kissed my nose, tore off his dress shirt, then shifted. A ripple of pleasure went through me. I never tired of watching Milo's magic in its purest form.

It was my magic now too. Milo let out a howl and bounded across the shore to join his father, uncle, and cousins.

He promised he wouldn't leave me alone for long. I smiled at that. With Milo in my life, I was never alone. He filled my soul and completed me. I watched him silhouetted against the moon. The next time he howled, it filled me.

Laughing, I kicked through the water. Milo kept to his word. A few minutes later he came charging through the woods. I hiked up my skirt and ran toward the valley.

I was no match for him, of course. Milo would catch me. Lust filled me and my laughter carried back to him on the wind. Oh, my wolf would catch me. I was counting on it.

UP NEXT FROM KIMBER WHITE

There is plenty more in store for the men of Wolfguard in 2020. In the meantime, sign up for my newsletter so you can be the first to know when Erik's story, *Heart of the Wolf* comes out!

You may unsubscribe at any time. Plus, you'll get a free ebook when you join. http://www.kimberwhite.com/newsletter-signup/

BOOKS BY KIMBER WHITE

Wolfguard Protectors

Shift of Fate

Echo of Magic

Kiss of Midnight

Heart of the Wolf

Secret of the Fae

Dragonkeepers Series Page

Kissed by Fire

Tempted by Fire

Marked by Fire

Claimed by Fire

Freed by Fire

Mammoth Forest Wolves Series Page

Liam

Mac

Gunnar

Payne

Jagger

Wild Ridge Bears Series Page

Lord of the Bears

Outlaw of the Bears

Rebel of the Bears

Curse of the Bears

Last of the Bears

Wild Lake Wolves Series Page

Rogue Alpha

Dark Wolf

Primal Heat

Savage Moon

Hunter's Heart

Wild Hearts

Stolen Mate

Claimed by the Pack Series Page

The Alpha's Mark

Sweet Submission

Rising Heat

Pack Wars

Choosing an Alpha

The Complete Series Box Set

ABOUT THE AUTHOR

Kimber White writes steamy paranormal romance with smoldering, alpha male shifters and kickass heroines (doormats need not apply). She lives on a lake in the Irish Hills of Michigan with one neurotic dog, her sweet, handsome son, her fire-breathing warrior-princess of a daughter, and the most supportive husband any writer could hope to have (seriously, he just took said son, daughter, and dog out for a boat ride so she could finish this book in peace!).

She loves connecting with readers. Sign up for her newsletter for the latest word on her new releases. You'll get a free ebook as a welcome gift.

http://www.kimberwhite.com/newsletter-signup

Made in the USA
Monee, IL
18 July 2020

36714565R00121